### A Colt Is a Great Convincer . . .

York took a deep breath and balled his fists. "You ain't seen anything yet, lawman. I'm going to stomp your ass into the dirt!"

Longarm had had just about enough. He was sure that he could whip York, but he was also sure that he'd suffer a lot of punishment in the process. So he yanked out his Colt .44 and shoved it right up between the brawler's eyes. "You want to die? Is your stupid pride *that* important, Mr. York?"

York's nose was bent sideways and gushing blood. His eyes burned with hatred but he was not insane, and when he measured the man before him he wisely decided that Longarm was not running a bluff.

"I'll have your gawdamn badge for this!" he gasped.

"Take it up with the town marshal or the mayor . . . but I work for the federal government and I don't give a damn what they say and neither does my boss. So are we going to have a conversation . . . or a funeral?"

# TABOR EVANS

# LONGARM

## AND THE BETRAYED BRIDE

JOVE BOOKS, NEW YORK

**THE BERKLEY PUBLISHING GROUP**
**Published by the Penguin Group**
**Penguin Group (USA) Inc.**
**375 Hudson Street, New York, New York 10014, USA**
Penguin Group (Canada), 90 Eglinton Avenue East, Suite 700, Toronto, Ontario M4P 2Y3, Canada
(a division of Pearson Penguin Canada Inc.)
Penguin Books Ltd., 80 Strand, London WC2R 0RL, England
Penguin Group Ireland, 25 St. Stephen's Green, Dublin 2, Ireland (a division of Penguin Books Ltd.)
Penguin Group (Australia), 250 Camberwell Road, Camberwell, Victoria 3124, Australia
(a division of Pearson Australia Group Pty. Ltd.)
Penguin Books India Pvt. Ltd., 11 Community Centre, Panchsheel Park, New Delhi—110 017, India
Penguin Group (NZ), 67 Apollo Drive, Rosedale, North Shore 0632, New Zealand
(a division of Pearson New Zealand Ltd.)
Penguin Books (South Africa) (Pty.) Ltd., 24 Sturdee Avenue, Rosebank, Johannesburg 2196,
South Africa

Penguin Books Ltd., Registered Offices: 80 Strand, London WC2R 0RL, England

LONGARM AND THE BETRAYED BRIDE

A Jove Book / published by arrangement with the author

PRINTING HISTORY
Jove edition / March 2011

ISBN: 978-0-515-14905-0

JOVE®
Jove Books are published by The Berkley Publishing Group,
a division of Penguin Group (USA) Inc.,
375 Hudson Street, New York, New York 10014.
JOVE® is a registered trademark of Penguin Group (USA) Inc.
The "J" design is a trademark of Penguin Group (USA) Inc.

PRINTED IN THE UNITED STATES OF AMERICA

10  9  8  7  6  5  4  3  2  1

# Chapter 1

"It was one hell of a nice ceremony," Billy Vail said as they stood side by side drinking champagne and watching the wedding crowd dance. "You know what?"

"What?" Longarm asked, his eyes fixed darkly on the bride and groom as they whirled around the dance floor.

"I never thought that Alice would get over you and find a man whom she really wanted to marry."

Longarm's jaw muscles clenched. "I figured that your sister would find a husband sooner rather than later. She's too beautiful a woman to live out her life as a spinster."

"She is at that," Billy agreed. "But she carried a torch for you a long, long time."

"Too long. I never led her on, Billy. You know I wouldn't do a thing like that to your sister."

"I know," Billy said, his eyes a little glassy from all the champagne. "You're a rogue and a womanizer, but you're not a gold digger or a cad. Alice seems to have found herself a fine young man."

"Yep."

"It all happened so suddenly," Billy continued, raising

his glass for a refill. "One day Alice is mooning over you and thinking that she'll never find another love, and the next day here's this man Jesse Walker at her side with an impressive diamond engagement ring."

"He's tall and handsome," Longarm said. "Seems pleasant enough, and you've told me that he fit right into your family."

United States Marshal Billy Vail was Longarm's boss, and he was prosperous enough to foot the bill for this big wedding reception. So when he called for another glass of champagne, it was filled for both of them immediately.

"Drink up, Custis!"

"I'm drinkin', Billy."

"You sorry that you let Alice go?"

It was the very question that Deputy U.S. Marshal Custis Long had been asking himself all day. And when he looked down deep inside, he felt genuine regret and sadness.

"Yeah, Billy, I think I missed the boat with your sister. She was the best woman that I've met in many a year. I just . . . just wasn't ready to make the commitment, and when she said she'd like to have at least six children, well, that spooked me pretty bad."

"Six is a lot," Billy had to agree. "And I just don't see you as the kind of man who would like to bounce babies on his knee or help out feeding them a bottle of milk in the middle of the night."

"You're right," Longarm admitted. "I like puppies and kittens a whole lot more than babies. And little, screechin' kids drive me half up the wall. I'd have been a lousy father until the kids were older."

"Well, Alice's new husband says that he loves children and wants at least ten. I think that was one of the things that really won my sister's heart. He appears to be a real family man."

"I'm sure that he is," Longarm said, tossing his glass of

champagne down and thinking that he needed his own full bottle.

Billy was grinning, and people kept coming by to offer him their congratulations not only on his sister getting hitched but also on the fine reception. There was supposed to be music, but the two best fiddlers in all of Denver had gotten drunk early during the wedding ceremony and still weren't sober enough to play, so they'd found a couple of guys who could strum the guitar and sing. Even so, with the champagne flowing, people seemed not to notice the poor music as they danced and laughed.

"Yeah," Billy was saying, "as soon as Alice told us that she was serious about Jesse we invited him over to the house for dinner and enjoyed him tremendously. He's a very well-spoken and pleasant young man. Comes from a very prosperous ranching family in Nevada."

"He's obviously had some schooling," Longarm said. "And that suit he's wearing must have cost more than I make in an entire month."

"I think he's quite wealthy . . . or at least that's the impression he's given us. His family runs a big herd of cattle somewhere south of Carson City along the base of the Sierras. You ever been down that way?"

"Can't say that I have," Longarm replied. "I've been to Virginia City on the Comstock Lode several times and once to Carson City, but I've never ridden south of it."

"His family's ranch is located on the Walker River."

Longarm nodded. He, too, had met Jesse Walker and the man was polished and impressive but . . . but maybe a little *too* polished to have come from a ranching family no matter how successful.

"I'm going to really miss Alice," Billy said, his voice a bit slurred and sad. "And I'm sure she'll miss me and the family here in Denver."

"Of course she will."

"I just wish that she wasn't moving so far away. No telling when I'll get to see her again."

"You'll see her," Longarm said, thinking that *he* would never see Alice again.

"This all just happened so suddenly," Billy said, shaking his head in wonder. "One day she's broken hearted over you . . . the next she's in love with young Mr. Walker."

"I was wondering if they named the Walker River after his family," Longarm said in a halfhearted attempt at humor.

"Don't be bitter or sarcastic," Billy snapped. "Just drink up and have a good time."

"I'm doin' my level best."

"Well you sure don't *look* happy."

"Next time that young fella with the champagne comes flyin' by tell him to leave the damned bottle."

"You got a bad attitude today, Custis. Maybe coming here and seeing Alice getting married and so happy was a mistake."

"Probably was, but I'm here."

Billy signaled for more champagne and when the man came, Longarm yanked the bottle out of his hands and growled, "Find another."

"Yes, sir."

"Don't get drunk and quarrelsome at my sister's wedding. I'd be gawddamned upset if you did that."

"I'll behave, Boss. And while we're on the subject, you're getting a little drunk yourself."

"Yeah, it's a big day and I'm a sentimental man. But just . . . just try to be happy for my kid sister."

"I'm tryin'. Believe you me I'm tryin'."

Billy gave him a disapproving look. "Anyway, like I was saying, Alice sure got over you in a hurry."

"The heart can sometimes mend quickly," Longarm replied, trying to sound wise and profound.

"Yes, that's obviously true."

Longarm told himself to slow down on the drinking and quit thinking dark thoughts about Jesse Walker and how wonderful a time he'd have tonight with his new bride. "How did Mr. Walker meet Alice?"

"Damned if I know. I should have asked."

"Doesn't matter now," Longarm said, thinking he'd have a cigar and get some air outside.

But just as he was about to excuse himself and step outside, the miserable excuse for a song that was being played ended. Everyone clapped and then Longarm saw Alice excuse herself from her handsome new husband and come over his way.

"Hello, Custis," she said, flashing him that heart-melting smile. "I really didn't expect to see you here."

"You want me to leave?"

Alice was tall with lovely black hair, brown eyes, and a perfect complexion to match her perfect body. When she smiled, she could light up an entire room. Standing so close to her now, smelling the rose perfume that she wore, Longarm felt like the dumbest and most miserable man in the world for letting her go.

"Aren't you even going to congratulate me and Jesse on our marriage?" she asked.

Longarm made himself smile. "Congratulations, to both of you."

"Won't you come and meet my husband? I'm sure you two will really like each other."

"Maybe some other time," Longarm said.

"Would you like to dance?" she asked, studying him closely.

Longarm sighed, "I would be honored to have a dance with you, Mrs. Jesse Walker."

"Alice," she corrected. "Alice and Custis, just like it has always been between us."

"Okay, but it's all different now. As of today you're a happily married woman."

"And you're still a hard-boiled bachelor."

"Some things are just meant to be."

"I'm afraid that they are," Alice said, taking his hand.

Longarm passed his glass and bottle of champagne over to a waiter and caught Billy Vail's eye as he led the man's newly married sister out on the dance floor. Because everyone in Denver was well aware that the two had been "an item" before Longarm broke things off, the crowd quieted.

"Play something slow," Longarm ordered the pair of lousy musicians. "And keep your voices down because neither of you can sing worth a lick."

"My, my," Alice said, managing to smile. "You sure have a burr under your blanket today. I thought you'd at least be happy for me."

"I am happy for you," Longarm said, taking Alice in his arms as they began to dance. "But I'm just not feeling all that happy for myself right now."

"You're the one that made this happen."

"I hope that is not the case," he said, keeping his voice low as they waltzed around the floor and other couples joined in on the dance.

"And what is *that* supposed to mean?"

"Never mind," Longarm said. "Let's just have this one last dance together and let the past go."

"I have," she told him as she leaned her cheek against his chest. "But, Custis, you did break my heart."

"I'm a total idiot for that," he said. "But what is done is

done and I understand that you are leaving for Nevada on tomorrow's train."

"We are. I'm very excited about meeting Jesse's parents and all the rest of his ranching family. I sure do hope that they'll approve of me."

"I wouldn't worry about that even for an instant," Longarm told her. "They'll *love* you."

He heard a catch in Alice's throat and she whispered, "We have to stop talking or I'm going to start to cry and how will that look?"

"It would look just terrible," he said. "So let's just have this last dance, hold our heads high, and put the past behind."

Alice nodded her chin against his shoulder and sniffled. "Damn you, Custis! *You're* the one that I wanted to marry!"

"You probably got a much better man. And besides, I hear that he loves kids and wants to have a big family with you."

"Yes, he does."

"You'll have a good life in Nevada," Longarm told her.

"And what about you?"

"I'll . . . I'll get along."

"You be careful and don't get killed, Custis. I'd really be upset with you if my brother wrote someday and told me that you got yourself killed."

"I'll do my best to see that never happens."

"Promise?"

"I promise."

Alice tilted her head back and kissed Longarm on the cheek and he saw that there were fresh tears in her eyes. "Aw, Alice," he whispered, "I'm so darned sorry."

"Me, too, Custis. Me, too."

Longarm closed his eyes and they danced until the music stopped and he would have kept dancing but a strong hand was laid upon his forearm and a man said, "If you don't mind, Marshal Long, I believe I'd like to have the next dance with my wife."

Longarm opened his eyes and looked into those of Jesse Walker. "You look familiar. Have we met before?"

"No."

"You're certain of that?" Longarm persisted.

"Excuse us," Walker said in a not very friendly voice.

Longarm stepped away from Alice and the young rancher that she had just married. He had been at the wedding ceremony but hadn't sat close to the front and so had not really studied Jesse Walker. But looking at the man now, he thought he saw something that reminded him of trouble . . . even of evil.

"Good-bye, Custis," Alice said as her husband led her off to meet people.

"Good-bye,' Alice," he called.

And so she was gone from his life just like that and with ice forming in his heart, Custis Long quickly headed for the exit. Tonight he was going to get stinking drunk at his favorite saloon. Maybe he'd have to be helped to his apartment in the wee hours of the morning. He'd have a terrible hangover tomorrow, but it was Sunday and he didn't have to go to work.

No, all that he had to do tomorrow was try to put Alice out of his mind. Forever.

# Chapter 2

Longarm slept late the following morning, and his hangover was nothing short of monumental. But at least he had not embarrassed himself at the wedding reception because he'd left early. Left with a bitter taste in his mouth that no amount of champagne could wash out. Something was wrong about that marriage, and he knew it all had to do with the handsome groom, Jesse Walker.

Longarm made coffee and sat in his underwear, feeling completely miserable, although he could see out his window that this was going to be a fine day. What was bothering him so much about Jesse Walker? Was it just that he was jealous or envious of the man for being married to Alice? Or was it the fact that no one seemed to know anything about his background other than what he'd told them.

"Maybe envy is all there is to it," Longarm said, blowing the steam off his coffee and deciding that the best thing for him to do for his mental and physical health was to take a long, solitary walk. Walking cleared the mind and often lifted the heavy heart.

Longarm shaved, combed his brown hair, and got dressed.

He wore his standard outfit, which was a snuff-brown Stetson with a wide, flat brim, a brown tweed suit and vest, a blue-gray shirt with a shoestring tie, and low-heeled boots of polished cordovan leather. As for his weapons he kept a solid brass twin-barreled derringer attached to his watch fob and a Colt Model T caliber .44-40 on his left hip, butt forward. It was called a "cross-draw" rig, and although he was not blindingly fast, Longarm had proved many times that he could get his gun out faster than most and then shoot with deadly accuracy.

Before leaving his small but neat apartment he made sure that he had a couple of cigars in his pocket as well as a little flask of whiskey to take the edge off his hangover.

"I'll get some breakfast and . . . oh, damn! I promised Alice that I'd see her and her husband off at the train station."

The southbound left every other morning at ten thirty, which meant that he only had little more than an hour to be at the station.

Longarm took a final look at himself in his full-length mirror and shook his head at the dark bags under his eyes. He had not been sleeping well ever since he'd learned that Alice was getting married and leaving Colorado. Even last night his sleep had been fitful and poor.

"I've got to put the past behind and find a new woman to think about," he said. "But one that is the equal of Alice is going to be almost impossible to find."

Longarm locked his door on the way out and then descended the stairs to the first floor lobby. He nodded at one of his fellow boarders and stepped outside as the man was trying to start a conversation. Perhaps that was being very rude, but Longarm was in a hurry and not in the least bit inclined for idle morning conversation.

When he entered his favorite breakfast café, most of the crowd had already eaten and gone.

"Mornin', Marshal!"

"Morning, Ed. How about the usual?"

"Bacon and eggs, toast, fried potatoes, and hot coffee."

"Skip the potatoes this morning. My stomach isn't up to the grease."

"Did you tie one on good last night?"

"Yeah, I did. Went to Alice Vail's wedding and reception. Lots of people and plenty of food and champagne."

"French champagne will give you a bad headache every time," Ed told him. "You ought to stick to good old American whiskey or beer."

"I'll try to remember that."

"I heard that Miss Vail got herself a fine catch. A rich and handsome young rancher from way out in Nevada."

"That's what I'm being told."

"You meet him?"

"Sure. Even got to dance one last time with Alice."

Ed stopped and turned to study Longarm. "You brought Alice in here a few times, and I sure liked her. Maybe you missed the boat on that one."

"That's what I'm thinking. How about some coffee and we skip the talk this morning, Ed?"

"Sure thing. You do look to be out of sorts and I don't want to shoot off my mouth and lose a customer, but you should have been the one to marry Alice, not the rich fella from Nevada."

"Coffee," Longarm growled.

He was running a little late after breakfast and his long legs carried him swiftly along the sidewalk toward the train station. When he reached it, the train was still at the station and so was Billy Vail.

"Glad I didn't miss the train," Longarm said.

"It'll be pulling out soon," Billy replied, consulting his

pocket watch. "It's running a few minutes late as usual, but that's a good thing because Alice and Jesse haven't arrived yet."

"No?"

Billy shook his head. "They're going to miss the train if they don't get here in the next few minutes, and that's not like my sister. She's always punctual, and I've never seen her late for anything important."

"She's got some distractions now," Longarm said, trying to make light of the fact. "Maybe Alice and Jesse just played last night after their wedding and haven't been quite able to get here on time."

"It's just not like Alice."

"Maybe not," Longarm said, "but now it's Alice *and* Jessie Walker. New situation and new way of doing things."

The engineer blew the steam engine's whistle, and Billy began to pace back and forth on the siding. "I sure wish that they'd get here!" he said over and over. "If they miss their train, the railroad will make them pay a penalty for new tickets."

"I know," Longarm said. "But that's not your problem or my problem. This Jesse Walker has a lot of money, and I imagine he doesn't care all that much if he's penalized by the railroad. Maybe he's just having one last poke and it's too good to stop."

Billy Vail's eyes blazed with indignation. "Damnit, Custis, don't you dare talk that way about my kid sister!"

Longarm threw up his hands. "Sorry, Billy. Bad attempt at humor."

Billy nodded and started pacing again.

"All aboard!" the railroad conductor shouted. "All aboard!"

Billy was beside himself with worry. "They're going miss this train!"

"It's not your problem, Billy. Settle down before you

blow a heart gasket and fall over dead. If that happens, do you think that would make Alice or your wife and kids happy?"

Billy took a few deep breaths and then he raised his head as the train began to pull out of the station. "They've missed it. Can you believe they've missed their damned train!"

"I sure can," Longarm replied. "So I expect they'll catch the next one going out the day after tomorrow."

"I hope they're having fun," Billy said. "Because I'm sure not. I should be in church with my wife and children, not pacing back and forth on this train platform."

"Alice is a grown woman. She'll be all right."

"I hope so. I like Jesse Walker, but I don't really know the man."

"Go home," Longarm suggested. "My guess is that Alice and Jesse have overslept after a night of celebration and lovemaking. They'll catch the train on Tuesday and it won't matter at all."

"I suppose that's true," Billy agreed. "But this is not like Alice. You know her well. Do you ever remember her being late to anything?"

"No," Longarm had to admit. "I don't."

"They're staying at the Hanover House," Billy said. "I think I'll go there and make sure that everything is all right."

"They might think you're intruding. Acting the part of an overly protective big brother."

"But I can't just go home wondering why they missed their train!"

Longarm gave the matter some thought as they watched the train grow smaller and smaller into the distance. Finally, he said, "Tell you what, Billy. At noon I'll go to the Hanover House and see them. I'm sure they'll tell me that they just overslept and that they're not a bit upset with either missing the train or the fact that they'll have to pay a fine to re-book their train departure for Tuesday."

"Would you tell them that we were here waiting to see them off and that I'm awful damned annoyed?"

"No, I won't tell them that you're annoyed. But I will tell them that you are concerned and just wanted me to check up and see that everything is all right. And after I do that, I'll walk over to your house and tell you that everything is all right and you can stop fretting. My gawd, Billy, you're acting like Alice is your little girl instead of a grown-up sister."

"She has always been like my little girl," Billy admitted. "And I always was her big-brother protector."

"Alice doesn't need your protection . . . or mine for that matter . . . anymore. She has a husband whose job it is to love and protect her. We just both have to let it go."

"You're right. I know that you're right," Billy said without any conviction. "But go on over to their hotel and make sure that Alice didn't get sick or something. Once I know she's fine, I'll settle down."

"I'll go over there at noon," Longarm promised. "Then I'll come and put your mind at ease."

"Thanks, Custis."

"Don't mention it, Boss."

"You kind of loved Alice, didn't you?"

Longarm expelled a deep breath. "I did love her."

"Then why didn't you marry her and then you could both stay here and live?"

"Because I'm a lawman and I like what I do and that includes getting on the train and going to new country. I'm just not ready to settle down yet."

"Yeah, I know. And you're by far my best marshal and I couldn't get half the work done without you being willing to take on the dangerous cases and do the hard travel."

"So there we are," Longarm said.

"Shit," Billy swore, "things just never work out exactly the way we want, do they?"

"Never," Longarm told his boss as he walked away.

By noon Longarm was feeling much better. Not one hundred percent, but far better than when he'd first awoken. He entered the Hanover House and went straight to the front desk. "I'd like to pay my respects and congratulations to Mr. and Mrs. Jesse Walker this morning. Are they up and about yet? Perhaps having a meal in your dining room?"

"No, sir."

"Then I'll go pay them a visit in their room."

"They're not in their room anymore."

Longarm blinked with surprise. "Oh? Then they just checked out a little earlier this morning?"

The desk clerk at this elegant hotel was a man in his fifties with silver hair and a mustache. He was well dressed and carried himself like someone of considerable importance, which he no doubt was at the Hanover House. "Sir, may I ask what business it is of yours concerning this matter?"

Longarm hadn't been expecting this kind of question, but he understood that in a fine hotel it was probably unwise to give any information about house guests to strangers.

"I'm a friend of the bride and her brother."

"I'm sorry, but . . ."

Longarm bit back his annoyance. "All right then," he said, pulling out his United States marshal's badge, "how about this?"

The desk clerk studied the badge for a moment and nodded. "That is as good as any room key. But I'm afraid that Mr. Walker checked out of this hotel *yesterday* morning."

"What!"

"That's right. He left in hurry."

"Did he say why he was checking out or where he was going?"

"I'm afraid he did not, Marshal."

Longarm shook his head. "Mr. Walker married Miss Alice Vail yesterday, and they were supposed to spend their wedding night *in this hotel*."

"I knew about the wedding, but they did not spend last night here and of that much I am very certain."

"But I don't understand this," Longarm said, not bothering to hide his growing frustration.

"If I may be so bold as to make a suggestion?"

"Sure," Longarm said. "Anything you can suggest to clear up this mystery would be a big help."

"Marshal, it is unusual but not unheard of that a groom will give his new bride a surprise on their wedding night, and sometimes that surprise is not merely physical . . . but of another type."

"I'm not following you?"

"Sometimes," the desk clerk told him, "a groom might want to really surprise his bride and take her somewhere completely unknown and unexpected. Perhaps even exotic or exciting."

"Are you serious?"

"Oh, yes, sir! I've worked at this fine establishment for many years, and I could tell you many stories about wedding nights. And one thing I do know for sure is that they can be quite . . . unpredictable."

"So you're suggesting that Mr. Walker took his new bride somewhere more exciting or exotic to consummate the marriage?"

"That is exactly what I'm suggesting, Marshal."

Longarm thought about it for a minute. "You're sure that you could not be mistaken and that Mr. Walker might have simply switched rooms?"

"Not a chance. I'd know if that were the case."

"Is this hotel full right now?"

"Quite full. We cleaned and then re-booked Mr. Walker's suite yesterday afternoon. It is now occupied by a nice and well-to-do couple from Santa Fe. They are regulars and we were very happy to have that suite come up suddenly available because of Mr. Walker's early departure."

Longarm could tell that this man was neither a liar nor an ignoramus and that he knew what he was doing at the front desk. In this case, there was no mistake and no confusion.

"Do your guests have to sign anything to check out?"

"Of course. They make payment. Would you like to see the written record of Mr. Walker's checkout?"

"I would."

The desk clerk showed Longarm a ledger and it had a place where guests signed in and then a space where they signed out. Both signatures matched.

"I thank you for your time," Longarm said.

"I am sure that there is a very good explanation for the bride and groom checking out of the Hanover House one day earlier than you expected," the man said soothingly. "Nothing to worry about. When a handsome and healthy young couple like that gets married, they can and often do very . . . odd and unusual things."

"You should know," Longarm said. "Thanks again."

But outside when he lit his first cigar of the day, Longarm was suddenly feeling something was wrong . . . very wrong about all this. Billy Vail had been right that Alice was punctual and absolutely reliable and predictable. She would not have allowed her new husband to do anything stupid or foolish . . . even on their wedding night.

So where was Alice? And where and who was the man that she had married yesterday?

Longarm started walking and thinking. Something *was* wrong. He could feel it deep in his gut.

And now, he had to tell Alice's big brother . . . his best friend and his boss . . . and that was not going to be well received. Billy would come to exactly the same conclusion as Longarm . . . Alice was either already dead . . . or in deep, deep trouble.

# Chapter 3

"Alice and her husband are missing," Longarm said as he stood in the front parlor of the Vail home.

"What do you mean, 'missing'?" Billy exclaimed.

"After I left you I walked around a bit and then about noon I went to the Hanover House. The man in charge of the desk was there, and he told me that Jesse Walker had checked out *before* the wedding yesterday."

"That's . . . that's impossible!"

"I'm afraid that it isn't. The hotel desk manager says that it's unusual but not completely uncommon for a groom to stage a surprise for his bride on their wedding night."

"But not *that* kind of surprise," Mrs. Vail, a short, pleasant-looking women with long brown hair, said.

Longarm just shrugged his broad shoulders. "I'm only telling you what I found out today. The manager said that Jesse Walker did not say where he was going or why."

"How extremely peculiar!" Billy exclaimed. "Custis, what is your gut feeling about this?"

"Not good. But I don't think it's time to panic yet."

"We should check all the nice hotels in Denver."

Longarm shook his head. "I don't think that would be the wise thing to do. If Jesse Walker wanted to make sure that he and his new bride were not disturbed or visited, he'd simply register under a different name. We could spend days and never have a clue as to where they are."

"They have to be someplace," Mrs. Vail said.

"Of course they do," Longarm replied. "But my suggestion is just to wait until Tuesday morning, and if they also miss that train, then we start to worry."

"Do you think that perhaps someone might have mugged them? Possibly caught them going from the reception hall to the Hanover House and took them hostage?"

"No," Longarm said. "Remember that Jesse Walker voluntarily checked out of the hotel before the wedding. So he had to have had something in mind for last night."

"I'm sure that he had a lot of somethings in mind, but this is very strange and troubling."

"I know," Longarm said. "I don't have a good feeling about it, either. But the only sane thing to do is simply to wait until Tuesday morning and be there to see if they board the southbound."

"I'm not sure if I can stand waiting that long," Billy said.

"And I'm not sure if we have any choice. If Jesse Walker decided that he didn't want himself and his wife to be disturbed or visited until Tuesday, then I'm certain they can't be found."

Billy shook his head. "I suppose you're right. But. . . ."

"He is right," Mrs. Vail said. "We need to relax and just assume that everything is fine between those newlyweds. Let's give them some credit for having good sense."

"Alice has plenty of good sense," Billy said, "but I'm starting to wonder about this new husband of hers."

Longarm had the same uneasy feeling, but he didn't see any point in voicing that fact. He was, however, troubled by this nagging notion he had that he'd seen Jesse Walker someplace.

"Between now and Tuesday morning I'm going to do some nosing around," Longarm said.

"What kind of 'nosing around' are you talking about?" Billy asked.

"I'm not sure. But one thing I would like to find out is something more about Jesse Walker and his Nevada ranching family. Billy, you might consider sending a telegram to Carson City care of the local marshal there and asking him for any information concerning the Walker family."

"I doubt that we'll get any response. As you very well know, local law officials are not inclined to be especially helpful to federal officers. And if the Walker family is as successful and prominent as Jesse led us to believe, then they will be very unwilling to divulge any information about the Walker family."

"It's worth a try, Billy."

"Yes, you're right. I'll compose and send off a telegram immediately. I'll just say that the wedding was a great success, and we'd like to know if the Walker family would have a comment or something to put into our newspaper."

"That's a fine idea," Longarm told him. "In the meantime, I'm going to be asking a few questions. Do you know if Jesse Walker had any friends or business associates in Denver?"

"He never spoke of any. No, wait. I do recall that he was introduced to Alice by a local businessman." Billy frowned. "Let's see now. Yes, the man's name was John York, and he owns a popular stable somewhere in town."

"I'll find it and the man before the day is done," Longarm promised. "That's a good place to start. Anything or anyone else that you can think of?"

"Not at the moment."

Longarm was eager to be on his way. Maybe this was all silly and Alice and Jesse were having a wonderful time in some romantic little hideaway . . . but maybe there was something dark and treacherous underfoot. He simply had to find out, and he had to do it in a hurry.

"Keep us both posted."

"I will," Longarm promised as he exited the house.

"And be on your guard," Mrs. Vail called. "If there is something wrong with this young man from Nevada, it could be dangerous."

"I'm sure that he's everything we thought him to be," Longarm said, not meaning a word of it.

Longarm went to a popular saloon and had no trouble finding out that John York owned the Colorado Stables.

"What's this York fellow like?" he asked.

The bartender shrugged. "York is a hard man, but I've never seen anything vicious in him. Is he in trouble with the law?"

"No," Longarm said. "He just knows a man that I'm looking for. Is York honest?"

The bartender was an ordinary person with a full beard and sad eyes. "John is a horse trader. Have you *ever* known one that is completely honest?"

"No."

"Well, then you've answered your own question, Marshal."

"Do you know anything at all about John York?"

"Not much. He comes in here a couple of times a week. He's a big man and he has a loud voice. He likes to play cards and he's pretty good at it. Sometimes he'll pick up one of the saloon girls and take her out to a crib in back. I've never heard any complaints from them about him so I'm assuming he pays them fairly and doesn't abuse the girls."

"Does he have one that he particularly likes?"

"Yeah. Her name is Lucy."

"I know Lucy."

The bartender winked. "I'm sure that you do. Lucy is a favorite, but she's more expensive than the other girls that work in and out of here."

"I might like to talk to Lucy."

"You'll have to pay her, Marshal. Same as the rest of us."

"*You* pay Lucy for her favors?" Longarm asked with surprise.

"Everyone pays Lucy. And she's worth every penny."

"Will she be in here tonight?"

"Hell if I know. Lucy comes and goes as she pleases. She's an independent contractor, if you will. She's a cut above most of the working girls, and I think she's pretty smart. Smart enough to be saving her money so that she doesn't wind up working in a crib when she's old and ugly. Lucy doesn't drink too much and she's not into laudanum or any other narcotic. She's very selective about who she humps, and I think she has a lot of money in the bank."

"Do you know where she lives?"

"Of course. I've been in her bed. She lives in room number seventeen in the Castle Hotel just two blocks up the street. But don't tell her that it was me that told you."

"I won't," Longarm promised as he laid a generous tip on the bar top.

He left the saloon trying to decide if he should try to catch Lucy first or go to find John York. He knew where the stable was located because he'd passed it dozens of times. He also knew from its size that it was a prosperous business. York had a huge barn, dozens of corrals, and he was very prominent in his profession. Some of the marshals occasionally rented horses or buggies from John York.

"I'll see York first and then Lucy," he decided out loud. He bit off the end of a cheroot and stuck it between his teeth. Longarm sometimes smoked them, but he just as often chewed them when he was deep in thought and trying to solve some particularly vexing puzzle.

He found John York sitting with a bunch of his friends under a giant spreading cottonwood tree. There were six men and they were passing a bottle around and just in general having a nice time.

"Which one of you is Mr. York?" Longarm asked.

"That would be me," a large and well-built man in his thirties said. "If you're looking to rent a horse or a buggy, then you're out of luck. Everything is rented for today because of this fine weather. Come back tomorrow, though, and I'll make sure that my man Elmer takes good care of you."

Elmer was a little Irishman who tipped his hat.

"I need to talk to you in private," Longarm told the stable owner. "Won't take long."

"No," York said, his smile fading. "It won't take any time at all because you're interrupting my Sunday afternoon drinking and bullshit session."

"I still need to talk to you, Mr. York."

"Get lost."

Longarm inhaled deeply. There was just something about York that made the hair on the back of his neck bristle. He reached inside his pocket and drew out his badge. "Maybe you best change your mind, Mr. York."

York was angry at the intrusion. "Is this official business, lawman? Or don't you have anything better to do on a Sunday afternoon than to badger law-abiding citizens?"

"Won't take long if you get down from your pedestal and cooperate. If you don't, I'll have to take you to my office, and that is going to just ruin the entire rest of your day."

"Shit!" York spat. He came out of his chair and threw his cigar into the dirt. "This will only take a minute, boys. I'll be right back. And don't you drink up all of that bottle!"

There was some uneasy laughter and then John York marched over to Longarm and said, "Let's have it."

"Over here where we can talk in private, York."

Longarm didn't wait to see if the man followed him because he knew that York had no choice. When they'd walked over to a corral of horses, Longarm stopped, turned around, and said, "This is about your friend, Jesse Walker."

"Who?"

"Don't start with me that way," Longarm warned. "I know that Walker is a good friend of yours because there are people in town who have often seen the two of you together. So don't try to feed me any crap. I just want to know a few things about Mr. Walker."

York was as tall as Longarm and probably thirty or forty pounds heavier. He had a fist-flattened nose and his knuckles were scarred, telling Longarm that York was a brawler, possibly even a former bare-knuckles prizefighter.

"You can shove your questions straight up your ass, Marshal. I'm not telling you anything about me or my friends. Got it?"

Longarm could see that this was not going to be easy. He either had to back down and walk away, or he had to get physical. John York was making sure that those were the only two courses of action.

"All right then," Longarm said, reaching out for the man's arm. "I'm taking you in for questioning."

"Under arrest!" York exclaimed so loudly that his friends all swiveled around in their Sunday easy chairs. "What's the charge!"

"Obstruction of justice."

"I'm not obstructing anything but an asshole who is trying to throw his weight around and ruin my Sunday afternoon!"

"Come along, Mr. York."

Longarm knew York wasn't going to do that. Maybe, if there had been just the two of them the man would have reluctantly agreed to answer some questions, but given that he'd been drinking and all his friends were watching, he was in no mood to back down or show any sign of being cooperative.

"Get your hand off my arm!"

Longarm's fingers tightened and John York brought his knee up hard and fast. So fast that Longarm was barely able to pivot slightly and avoid having his balls crushed.

York drove a hard left hook into Longarm's ribs, and it hurt so bad that he wondered if they were cracked. This man could fight, and he was powerful! Longarm stepped back, blocked an overhand right, and shot his own uppercut into York's midsection. The blow was so well timed and hard that York actually lifted onto his toes. Longarm followed it with a left jab that sent the man backward into the corral poles.

A lot of men would have quit the fight then and there, but not John York. With a roar of anger he charged forward with his fists coming in at all angles. Longarm knew better than to retreat so he stepped in close, drove the heel of his boot down York's shin, and then hit him with all he had in the jaw.

York wobbled and tried to grab Longarm in a bear hug. Countering the move, Longarm butted the man in the face with his head and heard York's nose crack like a dry stick.

"Gawdamn you!" York shouted. "You busted my nose!"

"I'm going to bust a hell of a lot more than your nose if you don't give up!"

York took a deep breath and balled his fists. "You ain't seen anything yet, lawman. I'm going to stomp your ass into the dirt!"

Longarm had had just about enough. He was sure that he could whip York, but he was also sure that he'd suffer a lot of punishment in the process. So he yanked out his Colt revolver and shoved it right up between the brawler's eyes. "You want to die? Is your stupid pride *that* important, Mr. York?"

York's nose was bent sideways and gushing blood. He was bent over because his balls must have been on fire. His eyes burned with hatred, but he was not insane, and when he measured the man before him he wisely decided that Longarm was not running a bluff.

"I'll have your gawdamn badge for this!" he gasped.

"Take it up with the town marshal or the mayor . . . but I work for the federal government and I don't give a damn what they say and neither does my boss. So are we going to have a conversation . . . or a funeral?"

York glanced at his friends, who were staring in disbelief.

"Don't you worry about them," Longarm warned. "This is strictly between you and me. So what is your decision?"

York was breathing heavily through his mouth. "What do you want to know about Jesse Walker?"

"Everything you can tell me, and don't hold back because I'll know it and I'll arrest you."

York covered his face. "I need to get a wet towel and to sit down."

"All right."

They went into the barn and York found a towel. There

was a horse watering trough inside and he wet the towel and pressed it to his nose. "Where did you learn to fight like that?"

"I've toed the mark a few times."

"You ever fight for money?"

"No," Longarm said.

"Well, you should have because you could have made a pile. You hit as hard as any man I've fought. Were you really going to shoot me between the eyes if I didn't cooperate?"

"No," Longarm said, deciding to be honest. "But I'd have pistol-whipped you to your damn knees. I'd have made you talk to me one way or the other."

"Jeezus but you're a mean son of a bitch!"

"I am that," Longarm agreed. "Now it's time for me to start asking you the questions, and I'll start by asking how you came to meet Jesse Walker."

"I met him about a month ago. He came here and wanted to rent a horse and buggy. Said he was taking a beautiful young lady for a drive."

"Did you see her?"

"Yeah, but . . ."

"Describe the young lady."

"Tall. Black hair, brown eyes. Really a looker."

"That would be Miss Alice Vail . . . now Mrs. Jesse Walker," Longarm said. "Did you see them together again?"

"Sure, a lot of times."

"When was the last time?"

"Yesterday."

Longarm lowered his gun and stared. "Yesterday?"

"That's right. They rented a buggy and said they'd be back tomorrow night. I knew they were getting married and I figured they were going up into the mountains a little ways just to escape all their friends."

"And Jesse Walker paid you for the use of a horse and buggy?"

"*Two* horses," York said. "Two of my best horses and my finest buggy."

"And they didn't tell you exactly where they were going to spend last night?"

"The lady wasn't with Jesse when he rented the horses and buggy. I got the impression it was all going to be a big surprise."

"Well," Longarm said, "I'm sure it was a surprise. And I've got a big surprise for you, too."

"What kind of a gawdamn surprise?" York spat through the dripping and crimson towel.

"The surprise is that I am neither willing to bet that you ever see the lady again, nor Jesse Walker, and most important for you, Mr. York, I doubt very much if you'll ever see that fine set of matched horses and buggy."

"What!"

Longarm almost had to smile. "Yeah," he said, "I can see that this is just turning out to be a real shitty Sunday afternoon for you, Mr. York."

York's eyes burned. "Are you trying to tell me that Jesse Walker is a *thief*?"

"That and worse," Longarm told the man. "What do you know about his background?"

"He comes from somewhere south of Carson City and is part of a wealthy ranching family."

"And?"

"That's it, Marshal! That is all I know."

"Join the crowd, Mr. York."

"What is that supposed to mean?"

"I'm not sure yet, but I'll find out."

"If he's a thief, I damn sure expect you to get my horses and that buggy back."

"Talk to the local marshal about it," Longarm said, turning to leave. "That's your problem, and I've got a lot more important things on my mind."

Longarm left the stables, wiping the raw flesh on his skinned knuckles. He was convinced that John York really didn't know where Alice and Jesse were at the moment or that the man he had thought honest and even a friend was in fact . . . a liar, an imposter, and perhaps a murderer and a horse thief.

# Chapter 4

Lucy O'Hara still had her exceptional looks and good health. She was willing to admit to anyone who asked that she was a "lady of the night"—a courtesan. She was also willing to match her savings in the local bank against that of most anyone . . . even her most well-to-do customers. Lucy O'Hara was a woman who took no chances with the men with whom she chose to bestow her talents and considerable gifts. She would not go to be with any man who was unclean or unshaven. She would not take a man who was too drunk to perform and appreciate her performance.

When Lucy O'Hara sashayed into a saloon or simply went to eat, men stared and women glanced furtively at her, wishing they were half as beautiful, that their hair shone like Lucy's red hair, and that their eyes were of that special green that seemed to drive men into acting like silly boys.

Longarm was freshly shaved and bathed when he went to find Lucy. He met her walking down the street on the arm of a well-dressed young man wearing a bowler at a jaunty tilt.

"Miss O'Hara, how are you today?" Longarm asked, tipping his own hat. "Fine day it is."

"It is at that, Marshal Long."

Longarm was surprised that she knew his name, though almost everyone who got about downtown recognized him. "I'd like to have a moment of your time, if I may."

Longarm turned to the man on her arm and extended his hand, "And you are?"

"Mr. Smith," the prosperous-looking man stammered. "And if you'll excuse me, I was just going to say good-bye to Miss O'Hara and go about my business."

"Nice to meet you . . . I guess," Longarm said as the man hurried off. He turned to the woman. "It appears to me that I scared away one of your . . . clients."

"Oh, that's all right. He's a junior banker, and we were just coming back from shopping and the poor man was probably just embarrassed that you saw him with me. So, Marshal, at last we meet. To what do I owe the pleasure of this encounter?"

"I'd like to ask you about someone that you know."

"I know many men. None well," she said, giving him a lovely smile. "Who in particular are you interested in today?"

"Mr. Jesse Walker."

"Oh," she said, shaking her head. "*That* one."

"Yes, that one."

"What exactly did you want to know?"

"Is there somewhere we can sit and talk?"

Lucy glanced at the nearby entrance to the Castle Hotel. "Would you care to come to my room for a moment?"

"If you're not expecting anyone."

"I'm not." She fluttered her long eyelashes seductively. "I may be wicked, but I've always made it a policy not to work on Sundays. I'm sure the church ladies are certain that it's plenty sinful enough on the other six days of the week."

The woman said that with a laugh in her voice, and it

caused Longarm to smile despite the seriousness of his business. "I'd be honored to join you upstairs."

"It's well past noon and I'll have refreshments brought up," Lucy said as she went up to the hotel's entrance, which was immediately opened by a doorman who gave Custis a much-too-broad smile.

"Wilbur?"

"Yes, Miss O'Hara?"

"Please have room service deliver a nice plate of cheese, oysters on the shell, smoked salmon, crackers, and whatever else they have good-tasting in the kitchen along with a bottle of my favorite champagne."

"Yes, ma'am!"

"Miss O'Hara?" Longarm said, holding up his hand. "I'm just getting over a huge champagne headache that I earned from a wedding reception yesterday, so if you don't mind, I'll pass on that champagne."

"Then make it a bottle of good whiskey," Lucy told Wilbur. "Old Kentucky Home would do nicely. And some ice, clean and crushed."

"Yes, ma'am."

Lucy tipped the man extraordinarily well and continued inside where they crossed an impressive lobby with alabaster pillars and a polished marble floor. The desk clerk waved and Lucy waved back. Longarm got the impression that Miss O'Hara, although a courtesan, was extremely popular and well liked.

"I'm on the first floor down this hallway," Lucy said, leading them along a newly carpeted corridor. "Have you ever been in this hotel before?"

"A few times. Not many."

"It's a nice, safe place, and I've lived here several years. Wouldn't think of moving, and as long as I am discreet and tip all the hotel people exceedingly well, they seem delighted to have me as a tenant. And they look after my every need and welfare. Sometimes, I'm afraid that many men have fallen in love with me. They become . . . insistent and the staff here knows how to turn them away either with firm words . . . or, regrettably, with force."

"I'm sure they do," Longarm said. "From what I can see you are treated almost like royalty."

Lucy laughed. "Well, not quite. About a month ago they had the king of Norway and his wife staying here and everyone nearly fell over themselves trying to outdo each other's level of service. I think the poor couple was a bit embarrassed by the show.

"Come inside," she said, unlocking the door.

Longarm entered a very large and extremely comfortable parlor with its own fireplace. The furniture was a bit overdone to his way of thinking but obviously quite expensive. There were oil landscape paintings on the walls, and one in particular of the snow-capped Rocky Mountains was magnificent. Fresh flowers filled two vases and there were three separate doors leading off to what he was sure was a private bathroom and bedroom plus a large bedroom used for Lucy's clients.

"This is very nice," he said, meaning it. "About three times the size of my apartment."

"It's a pleasure to live here," she said, taking a seat on one of a pair of matching velvet couches facing each other with an ornately carved little table between them. "Please sit down. The whiskey and refreshments should be here momentarily."

Longarm removed his hat and sat across from this woman. Where Alice had been quite beautiful, this woman was not only beautiful but shivery sensual without even trying to be. Had she been well born, he had no doubt whatsoever that Lucy O'Hara would have been the wife of some very, very wealthy man. She would have been his show-piece wife.

"Now, let's get this unpleasant subject of Mr. Walker over with so we can enjoy a nicer conversation."

"Why is it so unpleasant, if I may ask?"

"Well," she said, sighing, "to begin with, Mr. Walker is anything but a gentleman. He is rude, boorish, and very rough."

This last word, "rough," caused Longarm to scowl in anger and worry.

"Is he . . . a man who abuses women?"

"Yes," Lucy said without hesitation. "But not physically, so much. I mean, when he is in the upper position he does use his physical power to intimidate and hurt you a little bit . . . but I was thinking every bit as much about how when he drinks he can become obnoxious and insulting. I only entertained him once and when he began to try to force me to do things that I did not care to do, I resisted. He became angry and profane. I ordered him to leave and he refused. For a moment then, I thought things were going to become very, very ugly and dangerous."

"What happened? How did you handle Jesse Walker?"

"With this," she said, reaching under a white silk pillow to display a two-shot derringer very much like the one that was attached to Longarm's watch fob. "He was hurting my arm, twisting it and being very nasty, but I broke free and reached under that pillow and brought my own little intimi-dator out for him to see."

"And that stopped him cold?"

"Oh, it did," Lucy replied. "And when I cocked back a hammer, he actually paled and started backing toward the door. As he was leaving he cursed me and said that he would 'get even.'"

"And you thought the threat to be real?"

"Very real."

"When did this happen?" Longarm asked.

"Almost one month ago. And ever since then I have kept a second derringer on my person where I can get at it fast."

"Where on your person?" Longarm asked without thinking.

"Would you really like to see where I hide it?"

Longarm decided that he really would and nodded.

Lucy O'Hara raised her eyebrows with surprise, then before Longarm could say a word, she unbuttoned her bodice, and there it was, a nice, pearl-handled derringer resting right between her lovely bare breasts.

His jaw must have sagged or even dropped because Lucy giggled. "My, but you act surprised."

"I am, a little."

"Well, when a handsome lawman asks me to do something, I guess I just naturally comply."

Lucy handed Longarm the derringer. "I've been told that it and the one I keep under the pillow are very fine weapons. But I'd like your opinion, Marshal."

"They're both of the same make and model and high quality." He checked to see that both were properly loaded. "I'd say that, if Jesse Walker had tested your word and will, he would probably have died here in this room."

"He would have," Lucy said. "When I was a girl, I had men who used me in the most harsh and cruel manner. Being young and kind of afraid of men back then, I suffered physically and mentally from their abuse. But by the time that I was thirty, I had gained the upper hand. Now, no man intimidates or abuses me . . . ever."

"Glad to hear that," Longarm said, thinking he had never met any prostitute that came close to matching this one in terms of the strength of her mind and the self-confidence and iron will she had developed.

There was a soft knock on the door.

"That would be our refreshments," Lucy said. "Would you please take care of it?"

"Of course."

The waiter was wearing a white smock and he carried a large silver tray laden with wonderful things to eat and a silver bowl with crushed ice and a bottle of Old Kentucky Home aged eight years. Longarm tipped the man generously and closed the door. He'd expected to see that Lucy had covered her bosom, but she had not, and Longarm being a gentleman he was not about to object.

"Now," she said when he had placed the food on the little table between them and poured the fine whiskey over ice, "what else would you like to know about that terrible man so we can move on to more pleasant conversation?"

"I want to know if he told you about his past. Where he came from and what he was doing here in Denver."

"He said that he and his family owned a large cattle ranch in the central valley of California."

Longarm almost dropped his glass. "*California?* Are you sure he said that?"

"Of course I'm sure. I've been to Sacramento and San Francisco, and we talked about some of our favorite places in those two fine cities." Lucy cocked her beautiful head a little sideways. "Please don't take this the wrong way, but you look absolutely shocked, Marshal."

He was more than shocked, he was *stunned*. "Call me Custis."

"All right, if you call me Lucy. But you do look more than a little surprised. Do you mind telling me what this is all about?"

"As I said outside, I got a little drunk yesterday at a wedding reception. The woman who was just married . . ."

"Let me guess," she said, holding up her glass and taking a sip. "Was your *lover*."

He shook his head with amazement and took a long sip of whiskey. "How did you possibly guess that?"

"It was easy. You're an exceedingly good-looking man and when I told you that Jesse Walker said he was from California, you were clearly shaken, which could only mean that you are very worried about the future of that bride."

"You're extremely perceptive, Lucy."

"I have to be in my profession."

"Also being stunningly good-looking doesn't hurt, either," he told her quietly.

"No, it doesn't," she admitted. "But I've known way too many beautiful girls who stayed in my profession just a few too many years. Tragically, girls with promise in my very short-lived profession are always wanting to build just a bit more of a bankroll before they go away where no one knows their past and attempt to become respectable. No matter how smart they are, almost always they promise themselves that they will go away next year and finally . . . they are old, or diseased, and they have no more good tomorrows."

"I understand," Longarm said.

"What was this woman's name that you loved?"

"Miss Alice Vail. She was the daughter of the marshal that I work for at the Federal Building."

"How old was Miss Vail?"

"Twenty-three."

"And still unmarried?"

"Yes, she had never been married. Alice was a very successful bookkeeper and quite an excellent portrait artist."

"Did she do a portrait of you?"

Longarm shook his head. "I'd never allow it."

"Why on earth not?"

"I just didn't want to have it, and I thought that she shouldn't have it, either."

"Because . . ."

"Because I knew that I was going to leave her if she pressed me to get married." Longarm drank deeply from his glass and refilled it without asking. "Lucy, *I'm* the one that is supposed to be asking the questions."

"Sorry." She didn't look a bit sorry. "So what is the matter if they were only married yesterday?"

"Well, in addition to the fact that you've just told me that Jesse Walker is violent and abusive and that he was from California and not Nevada . . . they *disappeared*."

"Disappeared?" She placed her glass of whiskey down on the table and speared a piece of smoked salmon with a toothpick, then added a cracker and popped them both into her lovely mouth.

"Yes. Alice's father and I had promised to see them off at the train station this morning. But they never showed up."

Lucy chewed thoughtfully. "That doesn't seem to me to be so troubling. Perhaps they . . . well, overslept, overindulged, or something."

"I don't think so. Jesse Walker rented a buggy and two horses from a man named John York. Walker said he was taking his bride away for a surprise wedding night."

"Perhaps he did just that."

"You met the real Jesse Walker. Do you think he is the kind that would do such a nice thing?"

Lucy refilled her glass, and when she bent over, her breasts hung like large, white melons, and Longarm impulsively grabbed an oyster and sucked it right out of its cold, white shell.

"I can think of many ways that Mr. Walker would surprise his sweet and somewhat innocent young wife, but none of the surprises would be pleasant."

"I think that the man is an imposter," Longarm declared, trying the salmon and a slice of Italian salami between crackers. "I don't know why he would put on such an elaborate ruse . . . but I think that is exactly what he did."

Lucy thought about this for a moment before asking, "Does the bride's father have a lot of money?"

"Some," Longarm said, "but he's a government employee and he's certainly not rich."

"Is he related to someone who *is* rich?"

Longarm swallowed hard as it dawned on him. "Actually, Alice's grandparents own a gold mine about fifty miles up in the Rockies and are said to be worth a small fortune."

"Then maybe that's it," she said, looking pleased with herself for bringing up this possibility. "I'd say it's more than likely that Mr. Jesse Walker learned about Alice Vail's grandfather being wealthy. And now . . ."

"He'll be after a ransom," Longarm said, snapping his fingers. "That may be exactly what will happen."

"Or," Lucy said, "tomorrow the newlyweds show up looking embarrassed and sounding apologetic, and nothing at all nasty or evil happened to Alice."

"I hope that's the case. Can you tell me anything more about Jesse Walker?"

"I'm afraid not. He is a very smooth talker and quite attractive . . . although I'd say that, in a more chiseled way, you are the handsomer man."

"Very kind of you to think so," Longarm said, feeling his cheeks warm. "And now that I've taken up some of your Sunday, I think I should probably be going and leave you in peace."

"I hope not," she said. "We have a superb bottle of whiskey to enjoy along with some delicious refreshments. And," Lucy emphasized, "you can't do anything about that girl until either a ransom note appears . . . or the newlyweds appear."

"That's true." He reached for another oyster and then for

the fresh pink salmon, which was as good as he ever remembered tasting.

Lucy jiggled her chest. "Do you like what you see?"

He swallowed hard, almost choking on the salmon. "Lucy," he managed to confess, "a man would have to be *dead* not to feel a stirring in his loins over those beauties."

"And you've been sucking on those oysters as if they were . . . well, these."

"Miss O'Hara," Longarm said, feeling a powerful hunger building. "You were kind enough to allow me to come up here and enjoy your hospitality. And you've given me some very good insight into what could be a cruel marriage and kidnapping for ransom. Now I really think you've given me more than enough and . . ."

"Shhh!" she urged. "On Sunday I never work . . . only play. Do you want to play with me, Custis?"

"Are you serious?"

"I am very serious, and I never take money on Sunday. Interested?"

His mouth was suddenly so dry he had to take a drink. "Hell yes."

Lucy's green eyes glowed. "Then let's see what you have and I have and see if they go together just as sweet and slippery as you please."

Longarm couldn't sit any longer. He jumped up and was embarrassed to see that there was a big bulge in his pants. Lucy began to undress and after that, things happened so fast and furious that they even forgot about the delicious refreshments.

By midnight, Longarm was completely exhausted and drained. He was giving it one last shot and Lucy was insatiable as she rode him as if he were a worn-out but still valiant stallion. "Come on, big boy! Give it to me! Give it to me!"

"Lucy, for gawd sakes, I already gave it to you a half dozen times or more and . . ."

She cried out, fell forward as she reached her own climax, and her voluptuous body shuddered. Kissing his lips, she gave her hips a shake, and her honey pot worked on him in a series of long, juicy contractions until Longarm was bucking and gasping. He didn't have a lot left to give, but he gave Lucy what he did have left inside, and she howled with delight and drank her whiskey straight from the bottle.

"Custis, you are a mighty, mighty man!"

"And you are a man killer in bed," he wheezed.

She handed him the bottle. "Are you complaining?"

"No, I'm addicted."

"Good! I want you every Sunday at least for the next month."

"I'm not sure I'll live through more than two Sundays."

"Of course you will. You'll have six days and nights to rest up between sessions and you'd better be rested and ready for me."

"I'll go crazy in between just thinking about how good you are," he confessed.

"Don't do that," she said, her radiant smile suddenly fading. "Don't think of me very much. Because one day I'll be gone, and I don't want you to be miserable."

"Where will you go?"

"To a secret place that no one knows about."

"And you'll never tell me?"

Lucy shook her head and her breasts over his face. "No, because then it wouldn't be my secret place anymore."

"I understand," he said, even though he was not sure that he understood Lucy O'Hara at all.

# Chapter 5

It was late in the afternoon when Jesse Walker drove the fine rented buggy and his bride into the little mining town of Gold Hill. The town itself wasn't much, just a dozen or so business buildings and a well-kept brick hotel with a white front porch and upstairs balcony. Jesse Walker had seen a lot of mining towns, and he could tell that this one had once been very prosperous but was now well into its inevitable decline. Besides the fine hotel there were still two saloons, a bank, a large general store, and a barber shop and livery. But it was obvious this once booming mining town had dwindled in population as the local ore production had declined. The good news from Jesse's perspective was that Gold Hill was no longer large enough to employ a lawman anymore.

That was going to be damned important.

"Jesse," Alice said, eyes wide with excitement, "you really surprised me by wanting to come up here to visit my grandparents before we left Colorado. They'll be delighted to meet you."

"Well," he said, "when they wrote to say that your grandmother's health wasn't up to a trip down to Denver for our wedding, I knew you were very disappointed, and so I decided that we ought to surprise them."

"Oh, they'll be surprised all right. Even more than I was surprised when we didn't get on that train for Nevada."

"I hope they won't mind us just showing up unannounced," Jesse said, pretending to fret.

"Of course they won't! I'm my grandfather's favorite grandchild. They'll be absolutely thrilled to meet you. And you're right, since we're going all the way to Nevada to live on your ranch, we might not have ever had the chance to see them again. They're both getting up in age, and there is no telling when they might pass away."

He patted her on the arm as if to comfort her from that thought and expertly drove the buggy up a steep hill toward an impressive Victorian-style house perched on the side of a mountain overlooking the town. This was an area thick with pines and Jesse knew that the winters up here must be hard. However, he wasn't concerned about the weather, only about meeting the rich grandparents and no doubt getting a sizable wedding present in cash.

"Tell me their names again?" Jesse said.

"Grandpa Elmer and Grandma May Wilson. They are the sweetest old couple you've ever met, and I know they'll love you."

"I do hope so," he said, grinning. "I'm going to be on my very best behavior during our short stay and I want to make a good first impression." He pointed off toward a mining operation located about a thousand yards to the east. "Is that their gold mine?"

"It is," Alice replied, her cheeks rosy with the cold air and the excitement of seeing her beloved grandparents. "My grandfather came up here at least thirty years ago and he was as poor as a church mouse. But he got lucky and struck it rich. He filed his claim, and he knew how to protect it from thieves. He can tell you the most awful stories about how claim jumpers tried to kill and toss his body in the river. Grandpa is old now, but once upon a time he was quite a man. He has wonderful stories, and he even had to kill a few men to keep what was legally his in this town."

"He sounds like quite a fella, all right. Is his mine still producing gold?"

"Not nearly as much as it once did, but the last I heard it was producing about a thousand dollars a month."

Trying to sound disinterested he asked, "Does your grandfather employ guards and miners?"

"Oh, sure. At least three or four. You can't leave a gold mine unguarded. And as for miners, he has some on the payroll but nothing like in the mine's heyday. Grandpa's mine has been producing for more than thirty years now. I don't know what its total production has amounted to, but it has to be in the hundreds of thousands of dollars."

"My goodness," Jesse said, clucking his tongue. "That *is* a fortune. Has he been pretty active in the town of Gold Hill?"

"He's been on all the boards and he's donated quite a lot of money to the town. He funded the building of the local school and I don't know what all else, but he's been a very generous man."

"I'm sure that he has," Jesse said. "I'm hoping that he'll be generous with a wedding gift of cash."

"Jesse!" she said, genuinely shocked. "We don't need my grandparents' money."

"I know. I know," he said quickly. "But money is something that you can never have too much of. Do your grandparents have children other than your mother?"

"Two others. Both boys . . . well, middle-aged men now. They live here and one owns the bank and the other owns that big general store we just passed. I guess you could say that the Wilson family owns most of the town of Gold Hill. But with the mines all playing out, the property values have fallen and Grandpa once told me you could buy the whole town for fifty thousand dollars."

"Yeah," Jesse said, "these mining towns boom and then they bust. I'm surprised that Gold Hill isn't a ghost town long before now."

"It would be if the mines were all worked out, but Grandpa says that some of the veins thread back for miles into the mountain. He told me once that he thought they'd be mining gold out of these tunnels for at least another hundred years. Maybe not fortunes, but still enough to keep the town alive."

"How about that," Jesse said, thinking hard. "Nothing like owning a rich gold mine, I guess."

Alice looked at her husband. "You might think mining gold is a lot easier than raising cattle and horses, but I doubt that's true. Have you ever been deep inside a gold mine?"

"Nope, and I don't want to be," Jesse told her. "There are a lot of mines on the Comstock Lode. Some of them go thousands of feet straight down and then the miners dig horizontal shafts under Sun Mountain where the air gets hot and steamy. Sometimes an unlucky Comstock miner will send the tip of his pick through a wall and hit an underground reservoir of scalding water. They get boiled alive so it's dangerous, even hellish work. I'd go crazy being that far underground. I like to stay on top of the earth where I can see the sun and breathe clean, fresh air."

"Well, it sure is clean and fresh up here," Alice said, inhaling deeply. "I'm really glad that we're taking the time to visit my grandparents before we leave for your family's ranch in Nevada."

"I wouldn't have it any other way, darling."

"Do you love me?"

"You know that I do," Jesse said, slapping the lines on the rumps of his team of horses as they strained to pull up the last few hundred yards to the Wilson family mansion on the steep hillside. "And I always will."

"Me, too," Alice said, eyes bright with happiness. "We're going to have a long and happy life with a lot of wonderful children."

"That's right," Jesse agreed. "At least a half dozen. And they'll all become cowboys and ranchers."

"Just like you, Jesse."

"Yep," he said, eyes taking in the mansion with a wide grin spreading across his handsome face. "Just like me."

They rode in silence the last short way up the steep and winding mountain road. Jesse could not imagine how difficult it would be to get up this grade if it were covered with deep snow.

Elmer and May were stunned to see their favorite grandchild married and standing at their front door with a tall, good-looking husband. May Wilson recovered first and threw her arms around Alice. "What a lovely surprise! We had no idea that you and your new husband were coming all the way up here to visit!"

"Oh, it was only a day's buggy ride," Alice said, hugging her and then her tall but aged grandfather. "And it really was Jesse's idea to make a quick visit here before we left for Nevada. No telling when I might get back this way again."

The two grandparents were beaming. Elmer shook Jesse's hand with a strength that surprised the younger man. "You're part of the family now, Jesse. We're very happy to meet you."

"Well, thank you, Mr. Wilson."

"Call me Elmer and call my better half May. Come on in!"

"I'd better tie up the horses and grab our bags," Jesse said.

"I'll have our houseman do that," Elmer insisted. He called over his shoulder. "Miguel! We've got company."

Jesse saw a short Mexican emerge from what he figured might be the kitchen. The man was in his fifties, solidly built, and walked with a pronounced limp. "Alice, I know that you remember, Miguel Escobar."

"Of course I do! How are you?"

"Welcome, senorita!"

"Senora, now," Alice said, showing the smiling houseman her wedding ring. "Mrs. Jesse Walker."

"Beautiful!" Miguel said, bowing and extending his hand to Jesse. "Congratulations, senor."

"Thank you."

"Miguel, would you please unhitch the horses and take them to our stable and feed, then rub them down after you've gotten the bags?"

"*Si*, Senor Wilson. It would be my pleasure."

When Miguel had left, Alice said, "He doesn't look a day older than he did when I first met him five years ago. I see that he still has a pronounced limp from that collapse in your mine."

"It's a miracle that Miguel is even alive. He was buried under rocks and rubble for two days before we could get to him. His leg was broken in four places and the local doctor wanted it amputated, but Miguel wouldn't allow that. He is much too proud, and I think he'd have rather gotten gangrene and died than to have to be a near invalid."

"Didn't he also have broken ribs and a pretty serious head injury?"

"That's right. Like I said, it's a miracle the man survived, much less can now do about anything he wants." Elmer Wilson grinned. "That Mexican is going to outlive May and myself. The man is ageless and we consider Miguel to be part of our family. But come on inside and sit so we can talk. We're very anxious to learn all about you, Jesse."

Jesse removed his hat and his eyes took in everything. What he saw was exactly what he'd expected to see in a wealthy couple's house. Expensive furniture, large oil paintings, lush Persian rugs, and impressive bronze statues. Nothing in this mansion was cheap, and it all must have cost a lot of money.

"How long can you young people stay with us?" May asked as they settled into comfortable couches.

"Yes," Elmer said. "The weather is good and we can take you around and show you all the local sights."

"That will take about an hour," May said with a mischievous grin.

"Oh, come on, girl!" Elmer protested with mock indignation. "At the very least we can give Jesse here a first-class mining tour."

"No, thanks," Jesse said quickly. "I just don't like to go where it's close and I feel pressed in."

"You'd get over that in time," Elmer assured him. "But how long can we expect to enjoy your company?"

"Only a day or two," Alice said. "And actually, this was Jesse's surprise. I thought we were going right to Nevada, but he insisted that we pay you a visit first."

"Well, well," Elmer said, sitting down next to his wife. "That shows more than words what a fine and thoughtful husband you have wed. So, Jesse, tell me all about you and your family."

"I'd rather talk about you and your family," Jesse replied. "I understand that you've had quite the colorful life in Gold Hill."

Elmer was pleased to talk about his life, and soon he was telling Jesse and Alice all about his wild, young days when he had nothing to lose and everything to gain. "There was no law in this part of Colorado. The only law was that of a

man's gun and his fists or a knife. Differences were settled
in blood. I know that because I had to kill three thieves
before I turned thirty-five."

"Don't let this story become gruesome," May said.

"It wasn't 'gruesome,' my dear. It was just that way, and
to tell you the truth, I fit right in here and everything I own
came with a fight."

Elmer Wilson had his juices up and he went on with
more stories but finally ran out of steam and stopped. "I
could go on and on, but that's the past and this is the present, so I'll just shut my trap and let you young people do
the talking for a while."

Jesse wasn't eager to have the conversation turn onto
himself so he said, "Well, sir, you've sure done well for a
man that started out as a penniless prospector."

"I was a fighter, but to be honest, luck also had a lot to
do with it," Elmer said modestly. "Luck and a lot of hard,
dangerous mining work."

"And," Jesse added, "the guts to stand up and defend
what you'd discovered and even to kill the thieves trying to
take it away from you."

"I've always regretted having to take human life," Elmer
said, looking genuinely sad. "But sometimes a man has to
do what a man has to do. It was either me or those three
thievin' sonsabitches."

"Elmer!" May protested. "Please mind your tongue!"

"Sorry, old girl." Elmer really did look sorry. "But those
three were bad to the bone and the world was better off the
instant I punched their tickets straight to hell. I hated to
take life, but in that case it was a favor to all of mankind
and especially to Gold Hill."

Jesse had listened to all of this talk, and he had judged
the old man to be the real deal. In his younger days, Elmer
Wilson would have been a threat, but now that he was

clearly in his eighties with failing health and eyesight Jesse didn't think the old miner was anything to worry about. Hopefully, Elmer's mental facilities were a little shaky, but his sense of generosity was still alive and healthy.

"I'm sure that you are very tired from your wedding and the long drive up here in that buggy," May said. "Alice, why don't I show you to your room and you can rest and refresh yourself."

"Thank you," Alice said, "I *am* a little tired."

"Run along," Jesse said. "I'll just sit here and visit with your grandfather awhile."

"Would you care for some of the best rye whiskey you've ever tasted?" Elmer asked expectantly. "It's a little earlier than I normally pour, but this is a very special occasion and so I'm going to make an exception."

"Rye whiskey would be perfect!"

Elmer Wilson struggled off the couch and headed for the other room for the bottle.

*I'll get the old bastard a little loaded and then we'll find out how much money he's going to give us as a wedding present.*

"Here we go," Elmer said, tottering back into the room with a tray, a bottle, and two beautiful crystal glasses.

"I'll pour," Jesse offered.

"That would be good. My hand isn't as steady as it once was."

"Well, mine is steady, and it gets steadier the more that I drink."

"Damn good to hear it," Elmer said affably. "It's going to be nice to learn all about you. Alice, you understand, is our favorite grandchild. We think the world of her."

"I'm sure that you do." He poured at least three ounces in each glass.

"My gawd!" Elmer exclaimed. "You do pour a full glass!"

"I do indeed," Jesse agreed. He raised his glass in toast and Elmer did the same. "To you and May and to Alice and myself. I only hope we live as long and as happily as a married couple as you and your wife!"

"Hear! Hear!" Elmer croaked, raising his glass and tossing half of it down in a single swallow. "To good fortune and to long-lasting love!"

Jesse drank, realizing that he needed to be careful and not get this old fart too drunk. But just drunk enough to get a very large, very generous financial commitment from him before supper.

Jesse was thinking . . . oh, ten thousand dollars would be a fair and reasonable wedding gift. Maybe, maybe even much more. If everything went as hoped, before the old man got completely drunk or his wife interfered, Jesse wanted a large financial commitment.

*Twenty thousand at least,* he decided. *This gabby and self-important old goat can afford that without batting an eye.*

# Chapter 6

That evening after dinner, Jesse and Elmer retired to the old man's small office with full snifter glasses of French brandy. Jesse could see that the mine owner was slightly tipsy but certainly not drunk. Now, he decided would have to be the time when the question of a wedding present had to be brought up although Jesse sensed that the subject required some subtlety.

"Have a seat," Elmer said with a smile as he eased into his office chair. "Did you enjoy the dinner?"

"Oh, yes," Jesse said. "Miguel is a fine cook."

"He is at that. Would you like a cigar?"

"Don't mind if I do," Jesse said. "Cuban?"

"How did you guess?"

"Oh," Jesse said, flattering the old man, "some men refuse to settle for anything less than the very best."

"Thank you," Elmer said. "And I can see that you're a man with excellent tastes, or you would not have recognized the rare and wonderful qualities of my favorite granddaughter."

"I'm a lucky man."

"We both are," Elmer said. "So how is the cattle business in Nevada?"

*Now was the time,* Jesse thought. "Well, I'm afraid that it has been a little rough these last few years."

"Oh, and why is that?"

Jesse Walker shrugged his broad shoulders. "My family owns a great deal of land south of Carson City, but I'm afraid that we've been in a prolonged drought. The grass has been poor and so our cattle have not done well. You couple a drought with three straight severe winters and it's been enough to drive a lot of the smaller ranchers under."

"But not you and your family's ranch I hope," Elmer said with concern.

"Well, Mr. Wilson, we are close to the brink. However, we know that we could weather this bad patch if the banks would lend us the money."

"How much money are you trying to borrow?"

Jesse had the sum in mind. "Twenty thousand dollars would do it."

"That's a lot of money."

"Not for someone like you," Jesse said quickly.

Elmer's eyes narrowed. "What does that mean?"

"Well," Jesse shrugged, "I was hoping that you and your wife might see fit to give your beloved Alice and myself that twenty thousand dollars as a wedding gift."

Elmer had been about to light his cigar, but now it was forgotten and so was the match in his hand until it burned his fingers and he dropped it into a silver ashtray atop his desk. "My gawd, Jesse, are you serious or just having a little joke on me?"

"I'm dead serious, Elmer. We really need that twenty-thousand-dollar wedding gift."

"You *are* serious!"

"Consider it as Alice's dowry if you will," Jesse said, trying to hold the smile on his lips.

"I consider it insulting!"

Jesse could see the old man's face was beginning to redden with anger. "Now wait a minute, Elmer. Maybe I was joking a little. Fifteen thousand would probably be enough to handle our ranching situation."

Elmer took a long drink from his glass of brandy and then he slowly lit his cigar and tossed a match across his desk toward Jesse. His eyes were bright with anger and his voice was cold when he said, "Jesse, what kind of a man are you? You marry my granddaughter and then you come here asking for twenty thousand dollars?"

"Fifteen will do," Jesse said tightly.

"I was going to give you and Alice five hundred dollars. That's the figure that May and I decided upon."

Now it was Jesse's turn to stare with shock. "Five hundred dollars? That's all?"

"I think," Elmer said tightly, "that we had better call it an evening, you and me. I'm getting madder by the second, and if we sit here across from each other much longer, I might say something I'll regret."

Jesse lit the Cuban cigar and studied the old man. *Five hundred measly dollars. What a stinking tightwad!*

"Then what about a fifteen thousand dollar loan?" he asked.

Elmer looked away for a moment. "I don't know anything about cattle ranching, and I sure don't know anything about Nevada livestock production. Why would a mine owner like me want to get into something that he is completely ignorant about? Do you think I'm stupid . . . or maybe a little senile with old age?"

"No, sir! But. . . ."

"Let me tell you something, Mr. Walker. Until just a few minutes ago I had thought Alice had found a wonderful husband. But right now what I think instead is that she married a con artist and a fraud. And tomorrow morning I'm going to tell Alice exactly what I think of you."

"That would be a big mistake," Jesse said, making a decision.

"Oh?" Elmer started to climb to his feet. "Well, gaw-damnit, I think I'll find and tell her right now what I think of you."

When Elmer started for the door, Jesse jumped up and blocked his path.

"Get out of my way, you . . ."

Jesse drove an uppercut into the old man's midsection. When Elmer gasped, Jesse grabbed him by the neck and twisted it violently one way and then the other. He heard a snap and Elmer Wilson went limp in his arms.

"Heart failure," Jesse said, carrying Elmer over to his office chair and placing him down carefully.

It took less than five minutes for Jesse to locate the strongbox hidden in the old man's office closet. Another three minutes to pick the lock and then grin at the sight of all the money and a huge gold nugget worth several thousand dollars.

He counted the money and it totaled almost eighteen thousand dollars. That much cash and the gold nugget would give him his twenty thousand.

Jesse looked down at the dead man sitting upright in his office chair. "You should have just given this to me and lived out the rest of your days. Instead, you forced me to do this the hard way. But that's all right. Comes out the same, doesn't it?"

Jesse looked around for a place to hide the cash. He saw and rejected a solid silver cuspidor and an ornate brass urn of some sort and instead decided to spread the cash neatly under the big Persian rug. No one would ever think to look there. He placed a hundred dollars back into the strongbox, replaced it in the closet, and dropped the big solid gold nugget in his coat pocket.

"Everything looks right to me," he said, lighting Elmer's cigar and placing it in the ashtray near the old man. He enjoyed his own cigar for a moment or two and then went to the office door, opened it, and yelled, "Help! Someone get a doctor!"

There would, he was very sure, be no doctor in Gold Hill. Maybe a tooth puller, but probably not. "Help!"

Alice was the first one to burst into the office and when she saw her grandfather slumped over in his office chair she screamed, "Oh my God! What happened to him!"

"His heart just must have failed," Jesse said, trying to look stricken with grief. "We were sitting here having a laugh when your grandfather grabbed his chest, cried out in pain, and then slumped over. I checked him, but he died almost instantly."

Alice covered her face with her hands and began to weep. May entered the room, and when she saw her husband, she threw herself at the old man, sobbing.

Two days later they all held a funeral and everyone for miles around Gold Hill came to pay their final respects. Elmer's two sons were stoic and were so shaken by the death of their father that they were nearly mutes. Alice seemed never to stop crying. May looked to be a hundred years old.

"Elmer loved his whiskey, brandy, and those damned cigars," May cried. "When we had a doctor in this town he told my husband they would be the death of him and he needed to quit drinking and smoking . . . but Elmer was his own man and he did what pleased him."

"He lived a full and rich life," Jesse said. "And he died quickly without suffering. I'm sure that he is looking down from heaven and smiling."

"I want to be with him soon," May whispered. "I don't want to live without Elmer."

"I'm sure that he is waiting for you with open arms," Jesse told her in a soft, comforting voice.

The funeral was short and the eulogy was surprisingly good. The preacher who gave it talked glowingly about Elmer Wilson and how much he had done for all of mankind and especially for those people in Gold Hill.

"Elmer Wilson was man that we all knew, loved, and respected. He put food on our tables, and he made all of our lives richer for his generosity. He will be missed but not forgotten. Ever."

Jesse stood with bowed head and one arm draped over Alice's shoulder by the grave as it was being filled, thinking about how Elmer Wilson had only offered him five hundred lousy dollars. And despite the long face he wore, inside he was laughing.

# Chapter 7

Longarm and Billy Vail had waited for the next train to leave Denver just in case the newlyweds were on board. But when neither Jesse or Alice Walker showed up at the station, they knew that something was very much amiss.

"I visited with John York at his stables early this morning," Longarm said, "and just like we expected, his horses and buggy are still missing. The man is furious."

"He'll never see either the horses or the buggy again," Billy predicted. "Custis, what the hell do you think is really going on here? I'm worried sick about my sister."

"I'm worried, too," Longarm confessed. "This whole business smells fishy."

"I should have checked up on Jesse Walker's background. But when Alice suddenly announced that she was marrying the man and after I'd only just met him . . . well, I was hoodwinked."

"You and a lot of other people. Did you send that telegram to the marshal in Carson City asking about the Walker family?"

"Of course, but I didn't get a reply. Custis, I can't just sit around here waiting to see what happened to Alice and her new husband. Maybe they were intending to return the buggy and horses but were robbed and even murdered up in the mountains."

Billy looked like he was about to go to pieces and Longarm had to try and calm his boss down. "That's possible, but unlikely."

"Maybe not," Billy persisted. "There are plenty of highwaymen who rob and kill people. They'd have seen a handsome young couple driving a very fine buggy with two valuable horses. I think it's very possible something bad could have happened."

"If they'd been simply robbed, Alice would have gotten word to us by now. And if they were robbed and murdered, surely someone would have found the bodies."

"So . . ." Billy threw up his hands in exasperation. "So what the hell are we going to do? My poor wife is out of her mind with worry."

Longarm had been giving that very question a great deal of thought. In fact, it was all that he had been thinking about since Sunday. "Billy, I believe that the missing couple drove up to Gold Hill."

"All aboard!" the conductor called as the train blasted its steam whistle. "All aboard!"

"Maybe they did and went to see the Wilson family, and right now they're having so much fun there that they just haven't seen fit to leave yet," Billy offered. "Elmer and May Wilson are extraordinary hosts. I'll just bet that Alice and Jesse are still at their mansion."

"You're probably right," Longarm said without any conviction. "But we can get up there and find out, can't we?"

"We can and we should," Billy said as the southbound train pulled out of the station. "Let's rent horses and get moving."

"Good idea," Longarm said. "But we'd better not go to John York's Colorado Stables. I think the man would insist on accompanying us up to Gold Hill and that would be an unwelcome development. York is so angry that he just might shoot Jesse Walker on sight."

"If I didn't do it first," Billy vowed. "We'll rent saddle horses at Ike's Livery."

"Fair enough," Longarm agreed. "Go home, tell your wife our plans, and grab what you need. I'll meet you there in an hour."

Billy nodded and took off. Longarm headed back to his own apartment to get a few things to travel with, knowing full well that he might be gone much longer than expected. If Jesse Walker had conned them all with the intention of doing harm to Alice and getting money from her grandparents, then the trail he must take in order to save Alice might lead all the way to Nevada and perhaps even to the great central valley of California.

# Chapter 8

Jesse Walker had been thinking a great deal about what he'd done and what he needed to do next to keep from getting his neck stretched. Rich old Elmer Wilson hadn't been the first man that he'd killed, but he had been by far the most profitable. And yet . . . yet Jesse was saddened that it had come down to breaking the old man's neck. If Elmer would have carried some real generosity in his heart, the wealthy mine owner would still be alive. However, he'd been shockingly stingy, offering only five hundred dollars as a wedding gift . . . hell, he'd been far worse than stingy. Miserly. That's what the old man had been and he'd died for that.

Elmer Wilson was a miser.

But now that he was dead and buried things were moving very fast. Jesse had a whole bunch of cash that he'd already collected from under the rug when no one was around. And he had that big gold nugget. The problem was that down in Denver two lawmen were no doubt wondering where he and Alice were right now and why they had not gotten on the southbound train the day after the wedding. Jesse knew that they would be upset and maybe even enough so that they'd start asking questions about him.

Those questions could lead the pair of federal lawmen straight up here to Gold Hill in a big hurry. Jesse wasn't too concerned about Alice's unimposing brother, but the image of the big Deputy U.S. Marshal Long was fresh and disturbing. Longarm, as he was called, was well known for his bravery and his ability to exact swift, gun justice. Thank gawd Elmer's body was deep in the ground and that meant that his death could never be questioned as being caused by anything other than a massive heart failure.

Jesse walked out of the cemetery knowing that he could not afford to spend any more time at Gold Hill. He needed to be on his way, but talking his new bride into leaving her grandmother still wrapped in grief wasn't going to be easy.

"Alice," he said when they got back to the mansion, "we need to talk in private for a few minutes."

"All right." Alice left her grandmother with her milk-toast sons, a banker and owner of the town's only general store.

When they were alone in their upstairs bedroom, Jesse said, "We need to leave right now."

Alice stared at him. "We just buried my grandfather! Why . . . why would I leave my grandmother so soon? She *needs* me."

"She's got her two boring sons at her side."

"But they're men and neither one is exactly the comforting kind." Alice placed her hand on her new husband's arm. "I really have to stay here and help Grandma May get through this sorrow."

"And how long do you think that might take to get her out of sorrow?"

"I don't know," Alice said. "But why the sudden hurry? Can't you see that we've all just had a terrible shock?"

Alice's words confirmed what he'd expected . . . Jesse was not going to get his wife to leave today. And maybe it was better if he deserted her now rather than later somewhere out in the West. Because sooner or later his eye would light upon another woman, and he'd want to possess her. Jesse knew he would soon be cheating on Alice and leaving her today at Gold Hill while he disappeared with all that cash and the gold nugget would be an act of human kindness. Something he could actually look back upon later in life and feel proud that he'd done the right thing by this lovely, incredibly naïve woman.

"Listen," Jesse said, desperately searching for some plausible sounding reason why he had to immediately go on the run. "I didn't tell you this before the wedding but I'd gotten a telegram a few days earlier saying that my little brother had been chasing cattle when his pony stepped into a badger hole. Bobby got hurt very bad in the fall and he's fighting for his life in the little hospital in Carson City."

"What!" Alice exclaimed, looking even more stricken than before.

Jesse forced an emotional choke into his voice. "My little brother Bobby could *die*."

"Oh my gosh!" Alice exclaimed. "Why didn't you tell me this when you learned of it?"

"And ruin your wedding day?" he asked, shaking his head back and forth. "No, I just couldn't do that."

"But we're *married*!" Alice cried. "It was *our* wedding, not just mine. Jesse, darling, starting right now we have to be honest and face life's trials and troubles together."

"Yes, of course you're right. I'm sorry. But I can't stay here any longer. I have to get back to Nevada."

"We'll go together."

"Can you do that?" Jesse asked with surprise. "I mean, you could come along in a few weeks and I'd meet you in Reno when the train arrived. That might be better, Alice."

She looked over her shoulder and he could tell by her

expression that she was caught in a terrible quandary. "I should be with you, Jesse. If your little brother . . . dies, then you're going to need my strength and support."

"He probably won't die," Jesse said quickly. "Bobby is as tough as a boot heel. And I can see that your grandmother really does need you here at her side. I just think this is something we have to do . . . for a short time."

Tears spilled down her cheeks. "Oh, Jesse! I'm so sorry about your little brother! Losing my grandfather to sudden heart failure is awful, but losing a young man like Bobby . . . that is even more tragic."

"I'll write letters every day once I get to Carson City," he promised. "Will you write me back?"

"You know that I will."

"All right," he said, making clear that this difficult issue was fully settled. "This just kills me but I'm going to hitch up the buggy and get on my way. Will you explain to your family why I had to leave so suddenly?"

Alice dried her tears with a silk handkerchief. "Of course, but why don't you take a moment and tell them yourself?"

"No," he said quickly. "They've already got enough sadness on them without adding my own problems. I'd really prefer to just leave and have you explain."

"All right," Alice said. "I'll help you pack."

"That's not necessary. Just go to your grandmother and let's say good-bye right here and now."

He kissed her tenderly and felt the tears flowing down her soft cheeks. *Yes,* he thought, *I am doing the right thing by Alice. It might take years for her to understand that, but I am.*

Jesse packed the eighteen thousand dollars in his bag and kept the huge gold nugget close in his pocket. He made one secretive trip back to Elmer Wilson's library and did a quick search just to see if the old man had squirreled any more cash in some hiding place. He didn't find more cash, but he did find a diamond ring and diamond-studded cuff links that would bring a small fortune in Reno.

"What are you doing in my father's library all alone?" a voice demanded, spinning Jesse completely around with the ring and cuff links in his hand.

"I . . . uh . . ."

"Those belong to my father!"

"Of course they do," Jesse said, feeling beads of sweat pop out on his forehead. "Your father said that he was giving them to me as a gift."

The banker, a small, pale, and bookish-looking man who wore spectacles, said, "I don't for a minute believe that because my father didn't even know you."

"That's not true, Willard. Your father and I got a little drunk the first night I arrived here and we established a real fine friendship."

"I still don't believe you," Willard said, his voice rising with outrage. "I think the reason that you are in my father's private library alone is that you are looking for things to *steal*!"

"No!" Jesse protested. "Willard, how can you say something mean like that?"

"Because there is something about you that rings false," Willard said, pointing a finger in his face. "I'm going to call my brother in here and we'll get to the bottom of this."

"Wait," Jesse pleaded, grabbing the man's sleeve as he started to turn and go for help.

"Let go of me!"

Jesse knew that everything was going to crash down upon him at once if he allowed this little banker to tell the funeral party what he'd just witnessed. Everything was going to blow up in his face, and it was going to be a complete disaster.

"Willard," he ordered, reaching for a silver letter opener lying on Elmer's big desk. "Stop!"

When Willard did not stop, Jesse took a long step after the man and plunged the letter opener up under his ribs and into the heart. At the same time he clamped his hand over Willard's mouth to kill his scream and dragged the dying man back behind the desk.

"That was a really, really bad decision you were making, Willard."

The town banker died with a shudder and Jesse shoved him under the desk where the body would not be seen unless someone went behind the desk, and that was not likely to happen any time soon.

Now, time was *really* running out. But as Jesse wiped away the blood from the letter opener and slipped it into a desk drawer, he rationalized that, all in all, it had been very good pickings here at Gold Hill. If he'd have had a few more days he might have gotten an even greater haul, but the old man had played the hand and it had cost him his miserly life and then Willard had bumbled into this place at just the wrong moment.

Jesse Walker had to leave now with the gold, the diamonds, and all that lovely cash. Better to go quickly before Marshal Custis Long and Marshal Billy Vail came roaring up the mountain from Denver to find Alice.

*Yes,* he thought, *much better and wiser.*

He emptied about three hundred dollars in cash from Willard's wallet and took his fine gold pocket watch and gold wedding ring. All in all, he'd gleaned about five hundred dollars from the banker's body. At the library door he paused and then said, "Sleep well, Willard. Sure wish I had time to pay a quick visit to your bank, but at least I'm certain that the citizens of Gold Hill will give you almost as nice a funeral as they did your skinflint father."

# Chapter 9

Mrs. Alice Walker saw her husband out of the corner of her eye as he was exiting a doorway and starting toward the livery where she knew he would be hitching up the buggy and leaving without a good-bye. Something inside of her ached at the thought of her handsome new husband leaving so suddenly, so she left her family and hurried off to kiss him good-bye one last time.

"Darling?"

Jesse Walker spun around in surprise, hand going for the gun on his hip. But when he saw his beautiful new wife he froze, then forced a smile. "I thought we'd said our good-byes and that you understood that I wanted to leave without tears or theatrics."

"I know that," she said, "but when I saw you out of the corner of my eye leaving like this to try to save your brother . . . well, I just couldn't bear to have you go off without a kiss for luck and farewell."

Jesse sighed. It really was a pity that he could not have taken this woman away. She was so lovely and loving that he knew he might never again find someone her equal. She *really* did love him.

"Maybe you could give me more than a farewell kiss," he said, finishing hitching up the buggy with the sorrels. "Maybe we could lie for a few minutes in that fresh pile of straw and give each other a really special farewell."

Her eyes widened with surprise. "You mean . . ."

He took her into his arms and began to unbutton her blouse. "That's exactly what I mean, my dear."

"Oh, Jesse!" she protested. "What if someone should come in here and see us . . . doing it?"

"I'm willing to take that chance," Jesse said, leaning over to kiss the swell of her breasts. "Very much willing."

Alice wasn't so willing. Being modest by nature, she tried to make him be reasonable. "We could go back into the house and up to our bedroom, if you'd like. We could do it right now."

"No," he said, breath coming faster. "I think it would be much more exciting to make love on that fresh pile of straw."

But Alice shook her head and tried to push free. "Jesse, I know that you're much more experienced in these things and have probably had a lot of women in a lot of different ways, but I just can't do this kind of thing right now."

He didn't care what she could or could not do. She didn't know it, but this was the last time they'd ever have the chance to make love, and he'd be damned if he was going to forgo the opportunity.

"Just relax, Alice," he said, pushing her backward toward the pile of straw. "Once we get started, you're going to be so happy that I insisted."

"But I'm not comfortable with doing it here and now!" she said, voice rising with anger and anxiety. "Please! Let's go up to the bedroom where we won't have to worry about anyone surprising us. My gawd, Jesse, if one of my family saw us making love in the straw, I'd never be able to look them in the eye again as long as I lived!"

He was losing patience, and his desire was fever pitched. "You're my wife, Alice, and that means that you'll do as I say!"

"No, please!"

He backhanded her savagely across the face, and she would have screamed if he hadn't clamped a hand over her torn lips. Then, with all the brute force in him he threw her onto the straw, grabbed her dress, and yanked it over her hips. "This is the last time," he panted. "So make it good for me, Alice!"

She was moaning and her eyes were wide with terror as he tore off her underclothing and mounted her. "Lie still and just enjoy this, my dear!"

Alice reached up and raked his face with her fingernails. She fought him with all her strength, and because she was dry inside his thick member tore at her tissues, hurting her terribly. Always before Jesse had been a gentle and expert lover, but this man on top of her now, grunting, thrusting, and grinning so wickedly down at her face . . . it was like something foreign and evil was inside of her.

She beat her hands at his back and at the side of his face, but it didn't slow him down, and when he threw back his head and roared with ecstasy, she felt his seed flood into her body, and she wanted to push it back out but could not.

"There," he said, climbing off her and staring down at his glistening manhood. "That was my farewell gift to you and maybe out of it will come a child."

Tears spilled from her eyes and blood was in her mouth when she hissed, "The only thing that could come from being raped so cruelly would be a *monster*!"

"But it would be our monster," he said, laughing.

"There is blood on your hands," she said.

"I'm sorry I hurt your lips."

"That isn't from my lips." Alice saw something else now. "That gold pocket watch and chain belongs to Willard! I remember when my grandfather gave that watch to him on his twenty-first birthday."

"*Did* belong," he told her.

"What . . ." Alice's eyes widened in terror. "You . . . you murdered Willard!"

"I'm afraid that the fool gave me no choice. He caught me in your grandfather's library, and he was going to summon everyone in and call me a thief."

"You are a thief."

"Yes," he said, still kneeling over her exposed loins. "A thief and a liar and a murderer. But I'm also your lawfully wedded husband."

Alice's face was no longer pretty. It was bloody and convoluted in a look that could best be described as having been consumed by revulsion. "You . . . you horrible bastard!"

He reached down and wrapped his fingers around her throat then began to squeeze. "I'm sure that you would betray me at the first available moment, and I just can't let that happen, Alice. I'm so very sorry, but I need some time to get away."

Alice Walker stared up into eyes that held no pity, no humanity. She tried to scream for help but the hand on her throat was powerful and crushing. She flailed and fluttered in the straw as he bore down harder and harder. Instinct told her to fight with all her strength, but something in her brain told her *not* to resist, but instead to go limp in the terrifying moments just before she completely lost consciousness. If this monster of a husband thought her dead, he might stop strangling her before it was too late and she fell into a death spiral from which there was no hope of return.

And suddenly, Alice realized it was easy to relax, *too* easy, as an unfathomable darkness swept away her dimming sight.

# Chapter 10

Longarm and Billy Vail arrived on heavily lathered horses to find the Wilson family in a state of profound shock. The old woman of the house, Mrs. Wilson, was almost mute with grief over the loss first of her husband and now her son.

"Willard is dead," Miguel told them. "I found him in the library behind the big desk. First Mr. Wilson, then his son. Both dead."

Billy paled. "How . . . how could that . . ."

There were tears in Miguel's eyes and his voice held a tremor. "The patron, he died of a sudden heart attack. But Senor Willard, he was *stabbed* to death."

"Stabbed to death with a knife?" Longarm asked.

"No," Miguel said, shaking his head in sorrow and reaching into his coat pocket. "With this!"

The Mexican held out a silver letter opener that was caked with dried blood.

"Where is the body?" Longarm asked.

"Still in the library."

Longarm started off fast with Billy right behind him.

They found the body, which had been pulled out from under the desk and laid out on the floor draped with a silk sheet. Longarm saw at a glance that Willard had been murdered with a single thrust that had sent the letter opener under his ribs and into his heart.

"Where is Alice?" Longarm said, coming upright and with a grim look on his face.

"No one knows," Miguel admitted. "We have looked everywhere for the senora and her husband, Senor Walker, but they are not to be found."

"Did you check the barn to see if that buggy they drove up here is missing?"

Miguel's eyes widened, and he shook his head looking shameful.

Longarm and Billy rushed out of the library and headed directly to the barn.

"It's missing," Billy whispered.

"Then Jesse must have killed Willard and took off with Alice before anyone could find the body," Longarm concluded. "It's possible that she still doesn't realize her new husband is a murderer."

Harold Wilson, who owned the town's general store, appeared in the barn's doorway. "It's all my fault," he moaned. "I knew that there was something wrong with Alice's new husband the moment I laid eyes upon him. And now, he's robbed and murdered my brother and taken Alice hostage."

"How do you know your brother was robbed?"

"His gold watch and diamond jewelry are missing from his body."

Longarm thought a moment, then asked, "When was the last time you saw your brother alive?"

"About five hours ago."

"And Alice?"

"About the same. We just thought they had retired to their room to rest," Harold said.

"So they can't have much of a lead on us," Longarm said, turning to Billy. "With luck, we can still catch them."

"Not riding our played-out livery horses," Billy said, shaking his head. "As tired as they are from the climb up into these mountains, we couldn't overtake a lame burro."

"Then we'll swap for a pair of fresh horses," Longarm decided.

"I have two good ones you can borrow," Harold told them. "I haven't ridden them in ages, but they're both sound. And I can supply you with whatever supplies you need for the chase."

"All right," Longarm decided. "We still have a few hours of daylight so let's make the most of it."

Billy Vail nodded, his face set and hard. "I'm going to kill that son of a bitch when we overtake him and Alice."

"Not if I do it first," Longarm vowed. "The main thing now is to get Alice out of that man's grasp."

"I agree," Billy said starting for the door. "Let's get those fresh horses and ride!"

But just as they were about to hurry out of the barn, they all heard a low, choking sound.

"What was that?" Billy asked.

"Damned if I know. But there's nothing in this barn except grass hay and that pile of straw."

The straw shifted and Longarm's jaw dropped as he saw a hand poke up through the pile. A woman's hand!

Moments later they were frantically digging Alice out from under the pile of straw.

"Oh my gawd!" Billy said, quickly pulling Alice's dress down over her knees. "She's been raped and beaten!"

"Yeah," Longarm said in a voice he didn't recognize as his own. "But at least she's still alive."

Longarm scooped Alice up from the pile of straw and carried her out of the barn and into the house. When May Wilson saw Alice, she fainted.

"Is there a doctor anywhere in Gold Hill?" Billy cried out to the family.

"No doctor," Harold told them. "We had one a few years back, but he just couldn't make a living as our town's population fell."

"Get a basin of cold water and a washrag," Longarm said to no one in particular. "I don't think she's been stabbed, and if she'd have been shot, someone would have heard the gunshot."

"We'll take care of her," a woman said, stepping forward. "We'll get her out of that dress and cleaned up, but it would be better if she was taken to her room."

"All right," Longarm said, scooping Alice up in his arms. "Lead the way."

Two hours later and as darkness was falling, the women came down from the upstairs bedroom.

"How is she?" Billy asked.

"She's going to live. But she's been brutally assaulted."

"Did she tell us *why* her husband did this to her and where he might be headed next?" Longarm asked.

There was a pause and then, "Alice can't speak. Her throat has been damaged quite badly. She tried to talk, but she can't right now. She may never be able to talk again."

Longarm had heard enough. "Harold," he said, "there is nothing here that I can do for Alice. I need to find her husband and make him pay."

"Don't call him her husband!" Harold choked. "That . . . that animal murdered and robbed my brother. For all we know, he might even have killed my father!"

"That's why I'm not wasting any more time going after

him," Longarm told the man. "So get a grip on yourself, and let's go get those fresh horses."

Harold looked dazed and half out of his mind, but he did manage to nod his head.

"Custis, if we ride into the night, we might lose the tracks of that buggy," Billy offered. "Maybe we should wait to see if Alice is able to tell us anything tomorrow morning that will help us find Jesse."

"You can wait," Longarm said. "But I'm not."

"Then neither am I," Billy replied.

Longarm had to shove Harold Wilson outside. The man was so distraught that he simply wasn't functioning. No matter. Longarm and Billy both had one hell of a lot of experience tracking down and bringing men to justice. Only this time it was more personal than usual, and the justice might be meted out at the end of a rope.

# Chapter 11

"We'll put these livery horses up in your barn while we're gone," Billy Vail said. "We'll need a lantern to change saddles."

"I'll get one," Harold said. "And after you get my mares saddled we can stop by my general store, and I'll stock you up with some provisions."

"Did you say your horses were *mares*?" Longarm asked with a frown.

"That's right," Harold replied. "Something wrong with that?"

"No, I guess not. But I much prefer to ride geldings."

"Well, these mares are sisters," Harold explained. "I got them in trade for some goods that a couple of Utes needed real bad for their families. I haven't ridden either of them . . . I just don't have time to ride, but the Indians rode in on these two mares and told me they were sound and well broke. They're really pretty attached to each other. You'll like the looks of them. They're a pair of matched pintos."

"I don't care what they look like," Longarm told the

man. "Just as long as they're sound and have some speed and endurance."

"Oh, I'm sure that they do. They're a little on the small side for a man your size, but both mares are well built."

"Let's get them saddled and get on the trail," Billy said impatiently.

Harold found a lantern, lit it, and they trudged out to the barn, leading their Denver rented horses. "Sure is dark out tonight," Harold said, squinting up at the stars. "Hardly any moonlight. I don't see how you can follow any tracks."

"A buggy makes a pretty easy track to follow," Longarm explained. "As soon as we get the mares saddled and some supplies tied on we'll ride back to your father's mansion and pick up the buggy tracks easy enough."

"I hope you catch that son of a bitch and shoot him down like a dog," Harold swore. "Although I'd prefer that you brought him back here so we can watch the murdering bastard hang from a tree."

"We'll take him alive if we can, dead if not," Billy vowed. "But we're wasting time jawin' here. Let's switch these saddles and get to movin'."

Longarm and Billy dragged their saddles off their weary horses and carried them over to a big corral. "Hell," Longarm said, squinting. "I can't even see those two pinto mares."

"They'll come running over here any minute now," Harold promised. "I come out sometimes at night and give them a few treats. Sugar. Carrots. You know."

"Here they come," Billy said as the two mares emerged from the darkness at a hard gallop. They skidded to a stop right by the corral fence and rolled their eyes and snorted in fright.

"They seem a little skittish," Longarm said as the mares whirled and galloped off a few yards.

"They're not used to three men coming up to the fence

at night," Harold said. "But they'll warm to you real fast if you feed them. Here's a couple of carrots Just hold them out in your hands and they'll know that you're their friend. After that, I'm sure they'll respond well."

"How long ago did you take this pair in?" Longarm asked, eyeballing the spooky twins.

"Oh, I guess it was a couple of years ago."

"A couple of years?" Longarm asked. "You tellin' me that neither of these horses have been ridden in a couple of years?"

Harold shrugged. "Like I said, I just haven't had the time to mess with them any."

Billy took one of the carrots into his hand and held it out to the nervous mares. "Come on, girls. Come and get it."

Longarm grabbed a carrot and slipped through the corral poles and started toward the pintos. "We ain't got time to fart around tonight," he said quietly. "So let's have some cooperation here."

He could see that the pintos were small as were most Indian ponies. But, as Harold had promised, they were both stout enough and even in the poor light he could see that they were pretty and well matched.

The larger of the mares snorted and inched forward. It took the carrot out of Longarm's hand and chewed it up fast, then when Longarm tried to reach out and pet the animal, it shied away.

"Harold," Longarm said. "These mares are as jumpy as a frog in a frying pan."

"Just give them a few minutes to get used to you," Harold said. "They'll be fine."

"Not so sure about that," Longarm grumbled.

It took another twenty minutes and half dozen carrots to finally get the mares haltered and saddled. The pair stood side by side with humped backs and rolling eyes.

"It's the dark and the cold," Harold said. "If it was daylight and not so frosty tonight these mares would be falling all over themselves trying to get into your pockets for treats."

"Let's cinch up and get on down to your general store," Longarm said impatiently. "This is taking way too long."

"You take the taller of the two," Billy offered. "Because you're a lot bigger than I am."

"Okay."

Longarm jammed his boot in the stirrup and so did Billy. The mares trembled, with their eyeballs rolling around. The minute the two men got their right legs over the cantle, both mares exploded in a wild fit of bucking. Longarm managed to jam his right boot into the stirrup and grab for leather. The pinto mare he was riding slammed into the corral fence, and he heard Billy cry out for help. But it was all that Longarm could do just to stay on board the pitching mare as she shot across Harold's yard and through his garden bucking like crazy.

"Damn you!" Longarm shouted as the man crashed into a picket fence and knocked it down, then headed for a clothesline.

The mare was still bucking when Longarm tried to duck under the clothesline and didn't make it. The line caught him under the chin and snapped his neck back on his shoulders. The next thing he knew he went flying and hit the dirt hard. The mare vanished into the night still bucking and grunting.

"Son of a bitch!" Longarm shouted, stifling an urge to haul out his six-gun and shoot the vanishing pinto mare in the ass. "Son of a bitch!"

"Oh, gawd! My shoulder is broken!" Billy wailed as the second pinto mare went flying after its mate. "Oh, shit!"

Longarm hurried over to Billy, who was writhing in pain. "Damn it, Harold, hold up that lantern so I can see him!"

Harold lifted the lantern and Longarm saw that his boss and friend was hurt badly. Billy's face must have slammed into the corral poles as his body was thrown halfway through the fence. One of his shoulders was bent at a strange angle and so was Billy's lower right leg.

"Gawd damn those mares!" Longarm raged, turning his head to glare at Harold. "They're crazy as loons!"

"But those Utes rode them all the way from . . ."

"Two years ago!" Longarm shouted. "And who knows what those Indians did to make them calm enough to pawn off on you for supplies!"

"I'm sorry!" Harold said. "I thought they were broke!"

"The only thing broke is Billy's leg and shoulder," Longarm snarled. "Let's get him into your house."

Billy screamed when they gently picked him up and carried him into the man's house then laid him down on a bed. Longarm unbuttoned his boss's coat, then his shirt and surveyed the shoulder. "It's well broke, all right."

"How bad is my leg?" Billy asked, gritting his teeth through the pain. "Is the bone sticking out?"

Longarm took a pair of scissors from Harold's shaking hand and cut Billy's pant leg up past his knee. The broken leg was already swelling, but a quick glance at it told Longarm that the man had not suffered a compound fracture. "No bone showing, Boss."

"Oh, sweet Jesus!" Billy gasped. "It hurts like a bugger!"

"You got any whiskey or laudanum?" Longarm asked.

"I've got both," Harold said. "Down at the store."

"Then go get them both!" Longarm snapped. He was being hard on Harold, but the fool shouldn't have taken in two such crazy sisters. "And hurry!"

Harold nodded and bolted out the front door of his house. Longarm looked down at Billy. "I've had worse breaks, and you're going to be fine."

"Maybe I will and maybe I won't," Billy replied through gritted teeth. "But how am I going to help you catch Jesse Walker?"

"You aren't," Longarm said. "You couldn't ride no matter how much you tried."

"Damnit!" Billy howled. "I can't stay here! You need my help, and I have an office to run back in Denver!"

"They can take you down in a wagon in a week or two," Longarm said. "Since this town doesn't have a doctor, I'll get that leg splinted, and we'll see if we can get your shoulder set straight and then bound up tight."

Billy shook his head back and forth. "What a son of a bitch of a time for me to get hurt like this!"

"It'll work out all right," Longarm said. "This gives me even more incentive to catch Jesse Walker and make him pay for all the pain and heartache he's caused."

"What are you going to ride?"

Longarm sighed and gave the question a moment's thought before answering. "It's late and this whole thing has turned into a can of worms tonight. I think I'd better just stay until morning and take up the trail. By then the two horses we rode up from Denver on will be rested enough to go. I'll take them both so I can relay them as long as necessary to overtake Walker."

"I'd just give about anything to be with you when that happens," Billy said. "But you need to be real careful. That man is a *killer!*"

"Well, so the hell am I," Longarm told his boss.

# Chapter 12

Longarm didn't get much sleep that night. He was baffled and hard-pressed to understand how Jesse Walker could have pulled the wool over all of their eyes in Denver. And because they had been deceived, they had let the man into their lives and the damage he'd reaped was enormous. Old Elmer Wilson was dead, most likely murdered by the mysterious Jesse Walker. There had been a robbery in the house and that resulted in Willard Wilson being stabbed to death, and to top everything off, sweet and lovely Alice had almost been murdered in the barn.

Longarm supposed that Alice must have loved Jesse or she would not have married the handsome man who claimed to be the son of a prosperous Nevada ranching family. But how a man could so totally fool everyone was still something that Longarm was having a hard time wrapping his mind around. The only explanation he could think of was that because Alice had loved Jesse enough to marry him, everyone else had just assumed he was a good-hearted and honest fellow. But what he was in reality was a superb liar and murdering con artist.

No one knew how much money Jesse Walker had stolen from this house, but Longarm bet it was plenty. And there was talk of a big gold nugget that was now missing and that Elmer had always been eager to show off to his friends and family.

Longarm heard a rooster crow somewhere in the predawn and he knew that he couldn't wait any longer to begin the chase. So he dressed, checked his weapons, and gathered up his blanket, coat, and the rifle that Harold had loaned him for the manhunt. He tiptoed downstairs to the kitchen intent on getting some bread, meat, or whatever else he might shove into his coat pockets for the road because once on the chase, he would be missing a lot of meals.

"I knew that you'd be up before dawn and preparing to go," Alice offered in a raspy whisper as she slipped into the kitchen fully dressed.

She had surprised Longarm, and he turned around quickly. "Alice, you can talk."

"I found part of my voice deep in the night," she told him. "But not all of it."

"Enough," he said. "Do you have any idea where Jesse is going?"

"He said his younger brother Billy was hurt real bad at the Nevada ranch and that was why he was leaving so suddenly."

"I don't believe that," Longarm told her. "He lied about everything else so why should we believe that he even came from Nevada, much less a prominent ranch near Carson City?"

"I don't know," Alice whispered, wiping bitter tears from her eyes. "Do you understand why I'm still alive?"

"You shouldn't be talking."

Her voice was shrill and it broke. "I have to tell someone!"

Longarm found a knife and began cutting himself a big hunk of sourdough bread for the trail. Alice looked terrible with her lips all puffy and her face cut and battered. But worst of all were the purple bruises on her neck.

"I saw blood on Jesse's hands and then I saw that he'd taken Willard's precious gold pocket watch and chain. That's when I *knew* my husband was a thief and a murderer. And when I threatened to cry out for help, he grabbed and started choking me."

He carefully laid the knife on the wooden cutting board and turned to the tortured woman. "Alice, don't . . ."

"I knew I was about to die so I took a deep breath, held it in, and forced my body to become limp. He thought I'd died, and that's when he finally covered me up with straw so I wouldn't be found right away and left. I . . ."

Alice began to cry, and it nearly broke Longarm's heart to see such an innocent and loving person in so much pain. He wrapped his arms around her and held her tight as she sobbed against his shoulder. "I'll find him, Alice. I swear that I'll find that man even if I have to go to the ends of the earth."

"*We'll* find him," Alice said. "I can't stay here and wait. I'm going with you."

"No. That's out of the question."

"I'm going," she insisted, scrubbing away her tears. "With you or without you I'm going after that man. He killed my grandfather and my uncle, and it's my fault because I brought him here. It was as if I'd turned a wolf loose among trusting lambs. He *slaughtered* them, Custis! He lied to me and then he tried to murder me. I can't let that pass."

Longarm smoothed her hair. "In time, this pain will ease," he promised. "It won't ever go all away. I'd like to tell you that it would, but it won't and I can't lie to you. But I will find the man that you married, and if I can, I'll bring him back to Denver or here and we'll have a trial. Not much of one, but a trial all the same, and I'll personally put the noose around his neck and we'll haul him into the air kicking and choking. No quick death of a broken neck. Oh, no! That would be too good for Jesse Walker or whatever his real name might be."

"I'm coming with you," she insisted as if she had not heard a word he'd been saying. "Custis, I'm going after Jesse with or without you. Just tell me which way it has to happen."

He looked into her glistening eyes and saw the pain and humiliation. He also saw the stubborn, rock-hard determination. Alice wasn't bluffing, and she wasn't staying behind.

"You leave me no choice," he said. "But if you travel with me, you're in for a hard time of it. We'll ride hard and fast, and we won't let up no matter how far we have to go."

"You ought to know me well enough by now to realize that I won't complain and I won't quit."

He shoved the chunk of sourdough bread in his coat pocket. "Do you think there is any beef jerky or cheese around here we can take?"

"I'll get some and a few other things." Alice tried a smile that failed miserably. "You go get the horses saddled and ready to ride. Billy said that he'd pay Ike for them and their saddles."

"That's good to hear. No need for us to start out as horse thieves chasing a horse thief," Longarm said at a poor attempt at humor.

"He's not only a horse thief, he's a murderer, and I'm a betrayed bride."

Longarm wanted to ask Alice if she was even a little bit still in love with Jesse Walker and if, when they found him, would she have the slightest hesitation about shooting him on sight. But now was not the time or the place for such a direct question, so he headed for the door.

"Custis?"

He turned. "Yeah?"

"I don't mind dying at Jesse's hand. I almost did that already. But if you were to . . ."

He held a forefinger up to his lips. "Won't happen."

"But . . ."

"Alice, I promise you that I won't let him kill either one of us. Can you just find a way to believe that?"

"I'll try."

"Fair enough," Longarm said as he hurried outside into the cold mountain air and looked to the east for the first faint color of sunrise.

# Chapter 13

Jesse Walker knew that they'd soon find Willard's and Alice's bodies. And they'd also quickly realize that the old man's money had been stolen, telling them that Elmer Wilson probably hadn't died of natural causes but instead been murdered. So as far as Jesse was concerned he was going to be tied to three murders up at the mansion in Gold Hill. Three murders would earn him a vengeance-filled posse bent on exacting swift rope justice.

And then there was the matter of Marshal Custis Long and that other marshal who would take these murders personally and not rest until they killed or hanged him.

"I've got to get rid of this buggy and I've got to do it in a hurry," he said as dawn broke and found him driving along a poor track along the side of a steep mountain. On the downside of the road, the earth dropped away for hundreds of feet into the belly of a dark canyon.

That night had been cold, and his progress had been slow as he'd navigated the treacherous road. He'd only passed two freight wagons, both of them heading east toward Denver.

One of the freight wagons had refused to pull over and had forced Jesse nearly off the side of a cliff. Had he not already been in such trouble and worried about his horses going wild and knocking his buggy off the cliff, Jesse would have shot the freight driver dead.

Now, with morning light he was feeling tired and hungry and hoping to find a decent-sized mining town where he could swap this buggy and matched team for a fast-moving saddle horse and some extra cash.

About eight o'clock and when the air was still frosty, Jesse came upon a pair of young men walking on the road and when he came abreast of them, he called, "How far to the next good-sized town?"

The taller of the pair looked up at him and said, "Pinetop is only about three miles back up the road, but it's sure not what anyone would call a real town."

"That's right," said the shorter man. "Pinetop is just a little tent saloon and not much else."

"What's next?" Jesse demanded.

"Well, about ten miles farther up this mountain is a place called Green Valley. It's got a little hotel with a few rooms to rent."

That sounded much better to Jesse. "Does it have a stables where I might put up my weary horses?"

"Sure does." The taller one tried a big smile and he was missing several of his front teeth. "Mister, you wouldn't have a little spare money in your pocket for a couple of down-on-their-luck fellas, would you? We ain't even got enough money to buy food, and we're both mighty hungry."

The corners of Jesse's mouth turned down in contempt. "Are you boys a couple of worthless beggars?"

"We're *hungry*, and you look to be kinda prosperous, what with that fine team of matched horses and that buggy. I can see that you have a nice gold watch and chain. But

Barney and me, we got nothin'. Nothin' at all, and we *are* hungry."

Jesse growled, "I can't stand beggars. Step aside or I'll drive right over the top of you."

"Well, sir," the taller one said, yanking out a little pistol out of his coat then cocking back its hammer and pointing it at Jesse. "It seems that you are not a charitable man, so we're just going to have to teach you a lesson in charity. Right, Barney?"

"Right!" Barney produced an old Colt Navy and cocked its hammer. "Mister, raise your hands up high, climb down off that buggy, and then empty your pockets."

Jesse shook his head. "You're going to *rob* me?"

"Yes, sir. But we ain't killers and once you give us your money and other valuables, then we'll let you travel your own way."

Jesse Walker couldn't believe his bad luck. Here he was, way out in the forest and he was being robbed. He needed to stall and so he said, "You're going to take my horses and buggy, I suppose, and leave me on foot?"

"That's a nice pair of boots you're a-wearin'," Barney said. "Look to be just about my size. I'll trade you mine for yours."

"And ain't that a fine coat he's wearin'," the other man said admiringly. "Looks to be a little big for me, but it'll do just fine, I reckon."

"You're going to strip me clean, I suppose," Jesse said, putting sadness and resignation into his voice.

"You suppose right; now shut your mouth and climb down here with your hands up in the sky."

Jesse had a pistol on his hip that he could draw and shoot fast and also a two-shot derringer strapped to his right ankle. But his mind was really on a razor-sharp skinning knife hidden under the left side of his coat. With two guns cocked and trained on him at close range, Jesse Walker knew this wasn't going to be easy, but he found his blood was pounding more out of excitement than fear. Not that he was underestimating the danger. Oh, no! These boys were ragged, but they looked tough and desperate enough to kill him if he offered any resistance. But hell, they might kill him even if he did exactly what they wanted, and when they discovered how much cash he was carrying in addition to that gold nugget, Jesse realized he'd be shot for certain.

"Get down!" the taller one shouted, extending his pistol at arm's reach. "I ain't going to ask you again! Get down now or I'll put a bullet in your slow-movin' brain, mister!"

"All right," Jesse said in a meek tone of voice. "Just, take it easy, and I'll do exactly what you say."

"You bet your sweet ass you will!" Barney crowed, his eyes on the pair of horses. "Fine pair of animals you got pullin' that buggy. Ought to be worth a pretty penny."

Jesse kept his hands up in the air while his mind raced. Barney was distracted by the horses, but his companion wasn't a bit distracted.

"That's it; keep those hands way up high."

"Don't kill me, boys," Jesse pleaded. "You can take what I have, but don't take my life."

"We won't," Barney promised, "so long as you do what we say. Let's have your wallet. I can see the bulge of it under your coat so don't try and tell me it's not there with a wad of money inside."

"Oh, it's there, all right," Jesse said, smiling. "And you'll find that I'm carrying quite a lot of cash."

"You are?"

"Yes, I am," Jesse admitted with a deep sigh of feigned resignation. "And if you boys will just let me safely go my way, I'll give you . . . one hundred dollars."

"A hundred dollars!" Barney cried, eyes widening.

"That's right. More than I expect that the pair of you have made in the last six months."

Jesse stepped down on the road and planted his feet solidly in the dirt. He glanced out over the side of the cliff for a moment, then gathered himself inside for what was about to happen.

"You hear that, Marvin? The man says he'll give us *one hundred dollars*!"

Marvin nodded. "Oh, I heard him all right. But how much money do you have all together in that fat wallet of yours, mister?"

Jesse shrugged and thought, *Why not get them really excited and distracted?* "Well, since you're certain to find out anyway, then I might as well confess that I'm carrying over eighteen thousand dollars."

Both of the young men just gaped with disbelief. Finally, Barney blurted, "Holy shit! Are you kiddin' us, mister?"

"Nope."

The pair exchanged glances and Marvin started to laugh almost hysterically. "By gawd, Barney, we're rich!"

"One hundred dollars is a nice payday," Jesse reminded them.

"Not as big as eighteen thousand dollars!" Barney crowed. "Mister, get that wallet out of your coat and show us all that money."

"All right, since you boys insist," Jesse said, reaching across his body and slipping his skinning knife out of its sheath and then pretending to reach up for his wallet. "Here it is."

The skinning knife had a four-inch-long blade and when it came out in a blur from under his coat, Jesse used a backhanded motion to slash Barney's throat down to the neck bone. Blood gushed forth and Marvin staggered backward in horror, pulling the trigger of his pistol. Jesse felt a red-hot pain burn his side, but he knew that he'd only been sliced by the bullet as he slashed Marvin across the face, blade cleaving his nose.

Marvin screamed and staggered and Jesse went after him with the skinning knife, tripping the man down to the road and then landing with bent knees on his chest.

"No!" Marvin wheezed. "Please . . ."

Jesse's left hand slapped Marvin's hat aside and then grabbed a fistful of long, dirty hair. "I'm going to scalp you," he told the young man whose face was a sheet of bright red blood.

"No!"

Jesse laughed and with a quick and practiced motion, he cut a patch of Marvin's scalp from his head just as cleanly as if he'd sliced off a chunk of salted bacon. Marvin struggled and bucked until Jesse drove his knife into the man's throat and then climbed off to survey his grisly work.

Both men were still alive, but bleeding out fast. Their eyes were wide open and filled with terror, their arms and legs slapping uselessly at their necks and faces.

"I would have given you ragged boys that hundred dollars because I've been pretty lucky these past few days. I did have charity in my heart for you both . . . but you were *greedy*, and I knew you were going to kill me for the horses and buggy."

Barney made gurgling sounds in his throat and his lips moved. Jesse supposed that maybe the dying man was trying to tell him that they would not have killed him for the horses and buggy.

Didn't matter anymore.

Jesse Walker picked up their nearly worthless pistols and studied them both for a minute before he tossed them off the road and into the heavy forest. Barney shivered and his heels slammed against the hard-packed road for a minute before he died. Marvin tried to get up and come at Jesse. Amazingly, he climbed to his feet and staggered a few feet in Jesse's direction while his killer laughed out loud until he collapsed and died choking in his own blood.

Jesse dragged both men to the edge of the road and then he kicked their bodies over the side of the cliff. As the dead pair raced each other downward, Jesse mentally bet on which one would be the first to hit the trees and rocks far below.

Barney.

He called down to where they'd vanished, his voice echoed with a triumphant sound. "You boys made some big mistakes this morning when you didn't shoot me right away and then got greedy. I could see murder in your eyes, so I murdered you first!"

He then used the skinning knife to cut off a small branch, and he wiped out the tracks of their bodies and used the same branch to brush loose dirt across their already thickening pools of blood.

# Chapter 14

Longarm and Alice covered almost forty miles that first day out of Gold Hill. Considering the pain that Alice was in from her beating and given the high altitude that made it tough on the horses moving ever higher into the Rockies, Longarm figured that they'd done very well. But now, the shadows were growing long across the canyons and the air was starting to get a chill.

"It's time to make camp," he decided, reining his horse off the road and into an opening in the forest. "There's grass and a stream here for the horses to drink. I'll unsaddle and hobble them and we'll get a fire going."

"I'll gather some wood," Alice offered.

When she climbed off her horse, Alice was so weak and exhausted that her legs wobbled and Longarm had to grab her to keep her from falling. "Easy, there. Maybe we should have stopped and made camp a while back."

"No, I'm just tired, that's all."

"You took quite a beating back in the barn," Longarm said. "You really shouldn't have come along."

"I have to come with you," she insisted, pulling away

from him. "And if I can get a good night's sleep, I'll be stronger tomorrow."

"You're a damn stubborn woman," he said. "But you've got a lot of heart."

"My heart is broken," she replied, voice ragged and edgy. "I was married a few days ago to a man that I didn't even know and he betrayed and then tried to kill me." Suddenly, tears filled her eyes. "Oh, Custis! How could I have fallen in love with such a monster!"

"Love can make you blind . . . or so I've been told." He smoothed the hair back from her cheeks. "Quit beating yourself up over it, Alice. What is done is done, and there is nothing you or I or anyone else can do about bringing Mr. Wilson and his son back to life."

"Do you have any idea what this will do to May given her already poor health and advanced age?"

"I can't even imagine," Longarm admitted. "That sweet old woman looked like her world had ended."

"It had! She and Elmer have been married over fifty years! They were each other's universe. And losing Willard like that . . . well, I just can't get over what a tragedy I brought upon that household."

"Gather some wood before it gets dark on us," Longarm urged. "And try to put your mind on other things, or it will destroy you."

"The only thing that is keeping me sane right now is the thought of what I'll do when I find Jesse Walker."

"That might not even be his real name," Longarm warned. "And he might not be from Nevada or California. From what I can see, your husband was one of the most deceiving and clever bastards I've ever come across in addition to being a vicious and unconscionable killer."

Alice nodded numbly and headed off into the forest. Longarm watched her a moment, and although he wouldn't have told her so, Alice looked like death warmed over. He suspected the cause of it went way beyond the near strangling death that she'd very nearly suffered.

He took his own advice and put his mind to work on simple tasks. First he hobbled their horses, and then he unsaddled and bridled them and turned them loose in the small clearing where there seemed to be plenty of good grass. They'd brought a few pounds of grain, and he'd feed them out of his hat in the morning. But already, he could tell that they were very worn down. Longarm just hoped that he would be able to either capture or kill Jesse Walker before this time tomorrow.

They had eaten and spread their blankets beside the small campfire. Longarm looked over at Alice and saw that she was shivering. "You're cold, Alice. We should have brought heavy bedrolls for this high country."

"I know. I'm afraid that I'll be half frozen before morning." There was a pause and then she said, "Can I sleep beside you? We'd both be warmer for the double body heat."

"Sure," he told her, lifting his own thin blanket for her to scoot under. "Makes a lot of sense."

She snuggled in tight against his body, both of them fully dressed. For a long while neither said a word and then Alice broke the silence. "Custis, why did you let me go? Six months ago in Denver we were a pair. I thought we were going to have a future together and then you just . . . disappeared."

"You met Jesse Walker. Remember?"

"But I never would have given him the time of day if you hadn't walked away from me. And when Jesse came into my life, well, I was lonely and vulnerable I guess. Maybe I was on what some people call a 'rebound.'"

Longarm formed his next words carefully before he spoke. "Like you, I was completely taken in by Walker's smooth, steady stream of lies. The man acted like someone who had been raised well and with a lot of ranching money. Jesse Walker knew more about horses and cattle than I did, and he really seemed to know the country around Carson City and the Comstock Lode. So when he began to court you, I just told myself that he was a much better prospective husband."

She squirmed around to face him eyeball to eyeball. "Why would you think that?"

"Alice, we've been over this too many times already. I'm a federal lawman! A United States deputy marshal doesn't have much to offer a marriage-minded woman because we're often out of town, the pay isn't all that great, and the risks of getting killed are high."

"Your boss and friend Billy Vail seems to have done just fine for himself and his family."

"Yes," Longarm agreed, "he has. But Billy is smarter than I am, and he seems pretty satisfied sitting behind his desk most days and doing paperwork. He was a good officer in the field, but he was no longer a young man and he was eager for a desk job and promotion."

"Maybe someday you'll be ready to take things a little easier and accept a promotion," Alice mused.

"Not likely, if I even live long enough to retire from being a federal officer of the law. When that happens I think I'll probably end up joining the Pinkerton Agency or some other private agency that does about the same work that I'm doing now, only they get paid a lot better. Or, I might just open a little business buying and selling guns."

She smiled. "I can't see you standing behind a counter selling pistols and rifles."

"Me, neither, actually." He gazed up at the bright stars. "I've even decided that I'd like to see Australia and maybe Africa some day."

Alice laid her head on her bent arm. "Custis, I never heard you say that before."

"I have met an Aussie or two and they're fine blokes." Longarm grinned. "For some reason they call themselves that . . . blokes. They love their beer. Anyway, they were both from the Australian Outback, which they claim is a lot like our deserts in Nevada, Arizona, and California."

"Why would you want to visit their deserts when nobody even likes our own?"

"Good question," he conceded. "But they also said that Australia has some beautiful green country. In the northern part, it's almost tropical and they have kangaroos." Longarm grinned. "I'd sure like to see a jumping kangaroo some day."

"Did you know that mother kangaroos have little pouches in their bellies that are like satchels where they carry their babies for a while?"

"Really?"

"That's right," Alice said. "I learned that in school. And there are said to be poisonous snakes everywhere . . . the most poison in the world."

"I don't cotton much to snakes," Longarm told her. "Maybe I'd rather go to Africa and see the lions and other big game."

"I don't think I'd like to go to either place," Alice told him. "I haven't even seen all that much of America. Have you?"

"I've seen quite a lot of it. I was born and raised in West Virginia and I did some traveling around the eastern seaboard. I went to Florida where the beaches have white sand and the ocean is warm as bathwater. Been up north all the way to Canada and seen the geysers at Colter's Hell. And I've been down to Mexico and over to the Pacific Coast and walked some beaches in California."

"Was California as beautiful as they say?"

"It was pretty nice," he told her. "But it's already getting crowded with too many people. San Francisco is a big city now, and between it and the Sierra Nevada Mountains there is this huge, fertile valley where anything grows and where it gets foggy sometimes even in summer."

"I'd like to see it."

Longarm thought a moment. "Maybe we will. I'm thinking that, if Jesse gets away from us here in Colorado, then we'll chase him all the way to Carson City, Nevada. I'll track down his family . . . if he really has one . . . and if he doesn't, we'll try to pick up his trail, and it could very well lead us over the Sierras into California."

"Do you think we'll have to go *that* far after him?"

"I don't know," Longarm admitted. "We've been following his buggy tracks all day and they don't seem to be getting a whole lot fresher."

"He's moving fast."

"Yes, he is," Longarm agreed. "And he can do that because he's got two good horses in harness. We just haven't been making up as much ground on him as I'd expected."

"I've slowed you down."

It was true, but Longarm said, "Maybe a little. But even if I'd have gone alone I don't think I'd have overtaken him by this evening. Do you know when we'll come to the next town?"

"I'm afraid not," she said.

Longarm pitched a branch on the dying fire. "There's one called Green Valley up this road but I can't recollect exactly how far. I'm hoping to get there by tomorrow afternoon. If we're in luck, Jesse Walker will be holed up there getting rested."

"I wouldn't count on that. Jesse isn't one to let any moss grow between his toes. He's pretty high-strung and not the

kind to sit around. Besides, you told me that he'll be expecting a posse to be coming after him."

"Yes, he will," Longarm replied. "But then again he might
figure that as small as Gold Hill is, it would take some time
to gather up a fair-sized posse."

Something rustled nearby in the forest, and suddenly their
horses had their heads raised and their nostrils flared.

"What could it be?" Alice asked as Longarm jumped up
and grabbed his rifle.

"From the way those horses are acting," Longarm told
her, "I'd say it was either a bear or a mountain lion."

"Will it come after us or the horses?"

"It could." Longarm fired three shots from his Winchester into the forest. The shots echoed off the mountains and
then finally faded into the night. "Whatever it was," Longarm said after a while, "those shots chased it off."

"And maybe Jesse is just a little ways ahead and he
heard them and will know we're after him."

"Not likely," Longarm said. "I think Jesse Walker is still
almost a full day ahead of us."

"If you believe that those shots scared whatever it was
out there away, why don't you come back here under the
blankets?" Alice suggested. "I'm getting cold again."

Longarm did that and after he was under the blankets, he
felt Alice's hand warm on his flesh and exploring.

"Alice, what the hell do you think you're doing?"

She kissed his lips. "Custis, you *know* what I'm doing.
We've done it before. Remember?"

"But you're a married woman."

"I may have gotten married, but we both know that it
wasn't a real marriage in spirit or love. I'm not cheating on
Jesse . . . I'm just trying to forget him as best that I can, and
you could help me do that."

Longarm could feel his manhood starting to stiffen. "Are

you sure about this? I mean, given all that you've been through in just the last three or four days?"

"I need you real bad, Custis." She tickled the inside of his ear with her wet tongue. "You're not going to make me beg for it, are you?"

Longarm gently kissed her bruised and swollen lips. He wasn't completely sure this was the right thing to do . . . but when Alice found his stiff rod and began to unbutton his trousers, Longarm figured he might as well do what the lady wanted.

"Be gentle," she whispered. "I've had enough of being roughed up by men for the rest of my life."

"I aim to please," he promised as he shucked out of his pants and helped her to do the same.

In a few moments, they were coupled and making sweet, soft love. Longarm could feel her trembling when he first entered her body, but after a few minutes of easy movement, she began to relax and enjoy the experience.

"We were very good together, weren't we, Custis."

"Yes, very good," he agreed.

"Then why . . ."

He placed a finger over her lips and concentrated on giving her all the pleasure that she needed and deserved.

Sometime later an ember cracked out of their little campfire and landed on his bare butt. It burned and it formed a small blister. Yet, Longarm was so intensely engaged in the lovemaking with Alice that he didn't even notice until the next day when he sat down in his saddle and said, "Ouch!"

# Chapter 15

Longarm and Alice awoke at dawn, boiled some coffee, si-
lently ate a couple of pieces of sourdough bread for breakfast, and then quietly broke camp. It was cold enough to see
your breath and the sky was darkening, which meant that
they might even have to contend with snow before the day
was over. Longarm quickly saddled their horses while Alice
attended to her personal needs.

"How are you doing this morning?" he asked as he tightened the cinches and bridled their horses.

"I'm doing a lot better than yesterday." Alice gave him a
quick kiss on the lips. "I don't want to say anything that
might embarrass you, but . . ."

He laid a gloved hand on her shoulder. "Don't worry
about embarrassing me. Speak your mind."

"I feel like you reamed me out and then cleaned me
out."

"Ha!" Longarm crowed. "Reamed and cleaned you out?
Where did that come from, Alice?"

"My heart," she said. "You replaced something that had
belonged to Jesse. And you made it cleaner."

"I wouldn't mind if you needed some more cleaning and reaming tonight," he said with a chuckle.

"We'll see about that," she replied, giving him a bold wink.

Longarm finished with the horses and held one as Alice stepped up into the saddle. When he took his turn and mounted, he cried, "Ouch!"

"What's wrong?"

Longarm stood up in the stirrups and rubbed his backside. "Something huge must have bit me in the ass last night."

"A man like you should always keep his ass well covered," Alice advised him as she rode out of the little meadow and back onto the road.

Later that morning, Longarm reined his horse up hard and said, "Stop!"

"What is it?"

He pointed down at the road. "See those dark stains in the dirt?"

"Yes."

"What do you suppose made them?"

Alice shook her head. "I have no idea."

"Me, neither," Longarm said, dismounting and handing his reins to the woman. "But I intend to find out."

He knelt by the large dark stain and ran his hands back and forth over it until he had brushed away a thin layer of topsoil. He poked around in it a moment and then looked up at Alice. "It's dried blood."

"Blood?"

"That's right. Someone tried to cover a lot of blood up right here. And look over there. Plenty more dried blood, but it's covered better."

Longarm carefully examined the earth. "These two big stains could only have been caused by a lot of blood being let and this sure doesn't seem the kind of a place where anyone would stop and butcher a pig or a cow."

Alice swallowed hard and looked up at the dark clouds overhead. "What are you thinking?"

"I'm thinking about Jesse Walker and someone he met here." Longarm walked up the road about twenty feet. "Look! See these footprints?"

Alice dismounted and led the horses over to where he stood. "Yes. Two of them, I'd think."

"That's right. So we have footprints and bloodstains and those buggy wheel tracks. What does that tell us, Alice?"

"Jesse killed two walkers."

"That's right," Longarm grimly agreed. "And do you think that Jesse is the kind of a man that would take them to the next town hoping to find them an undertaker that would give them a decent and proper burial?"

"Not in a million years."

"So what would be the most likely thing that he'd do?"

"He'd try and hide the bodies?"

"Yep. Or pitch them over the side of this mountain and let them roll into that deep canyon where the only thing that would ever find them would be buzzards and wild animals."

Alice visibly shuddered. "Stay right here," Longarm ordered as he walked over to the edge of the road and peered down into the canyon. He walked back and forth along the edge of the road's nearly vertical drop-off and then he halted and squatted on his heels. "*This* is where he tossed them over."

"I don't want to see them!"

"You couldn't even if you tried," Longarm told her. "But I'd bet a year's pay that both of those bodies are directly below me and way down in that canyon."

Alice's fists clenched in anger and frustration. "What are you going to do about it?"

"Nothing I can do," Longarm confessed. "If we go to the next town and bring back a rescue party, we'll lose another day at least, and we still might not be able to get far enough down into the canyon to recover the bodies. I'd guess they are lying at least fifteen hundred feet below us."

"So we just leave them down there for the wild animals to eat?" Alice asked, her face reflecting distaste.

"If the next town has a sheriff, I'll tell him about these murders. Could be he or someone else will know who the two men were that were walking toward Gold Hill. Most likely not. And I'll mark the spot where Jesse tossed them over the side. I can't think of anything more that we can do to help those two poor souls."

"There's a storm that's brewing up there," Alice said. "I can feel the wind picking up."

"It's coming down from the north," Longarm said. "We've just got to find Jesse before these buggy wheel tracks are wiped out."

"Then we'd better do it fast," Alice told him. "I've spent enough time up in these mountains to know when a good storm is about to hit, and this one looks serious."

"I know," Longarm told her as he scooped up rocks and made a very noticeable pile. It didn't take but a few minutes. Then he brushed his hands free of dust on his pants and mounted his horse.

"Ouch!" he said, grabbing the seat of his pants. "Damn, that must have been one hell of a big mosquito."

Alice nodded but didn't smile. Her dark and troubled thoughts were on the two bodies that were lying far down in the gloomy canyon. In these hard times and given these difficult circumstances she had a feeling that the bodies would go to bones and one day the stream below would flood and carry even the bones away.

# Chapter 16

Jesse Walker drove his team of horses on through Green Valley and made another fifteen miles when he came upon the town of Red Butte. The air was bitterly cold and snow was starting to fly. Red Butte wasn't a place that he would have chosen to seek shelter from a snowstorm, but he could see that it did have a couple of small hotels and saloons. Added to that were two cafés, a saddle and harness repair shop, and a livery stable.

"This will sure as hell have to do," he said, chin tucked down against his coat and hat brim shielding his eyes from the blowing, swirling snow.

He drove right up to the big double doors of the livery and hopped down from the buggy. He didn't need to tie the horses, they were standing nose to nose with the door and plenty glad to be out of the wind.

Jesse yanked open a door just enough for himself to squeeze through and saw three men sitting next to a fiery red potbellied stove that had been separated by a low brick wall from the rest of the barn out of concern about a fire. A crooked and rusty tin smokestack snaked its way up through the barn roof, which was lower than most.

"Come in out of the storm!" one of the men called. "Where you comin' from in this bad weather, mister?"

"I got a team of good horses right outside the door that are half frozen and completely out on their feet," Jesse said. "I was hopin' that I might put them up here for the night."

"Be two bits for the pair," an older man dressed in a heavy coat and bib overalls and rubber boots said. "I got a couple of stalls for 'em, and they can stay just as long as you can pay."

The other two men thought that the rhythm was humorous, and they chuckled into their gray beards. Jesse saw no humor in the remark and just nodded. "Can I drive the buggy and team in here so we can unhitch 'em out of the wind and snow?"

"Cost you another two bits to store a buggy in here. They take up valuable space, you know."

Jesse was annoyed, then realized that it didn't matter. My God, he was almost rich with nearly twenty thousand dollars cash in his pockets and a gold nugget worth more than most miners made in a year.

"Fair enough," he said. "But you're gonna have to hold open the doors for me when I drive in. The wind is blowing straight at 'em, and it was hard enough just to open them a crack so that I could get inside."

Words were exchanged and the other two men by the stove reluctantly came to their feet to handle the doors. They looked to also be in their sixties and none too happy about having to leave the warmth of the stove. Jesse could not have cared less about their discomfort.

It took some doing to get the doors open wide enough to drive the buggy inside. The wind was ferocious and slamming straight into the doors. Once they were open, the big doors crashed against the barn walls, and Jesse had to give a hand just to get them turned back around so that they could be closed. The entire episode was difficult, and by the time they had it all buttoned up the fire in the stove had been blown out.

"Damn!" the owner swore. "This is going to be one hell of a bad 'un all right."

"Could be we'll get four or five feet of snow before this is over and done with," another said, relighting his pipe and then opening the stove door to try to get it rekindled. "Hate the damn snow. Seen enough to last me two lifetimes and a vacation in hell."

"Then why don't you leave this high country and do us all a favor and go down to Mexico or some hotter'n hell place like that!" the third old man said irritably. "You sure ain't decoratin' this country with your sorry looks."

"He ain't makin' it smell any sweeter, either," the owner said, "way he farts like a horse day and night."

"I can't help that, damn your eyes! I can't afford to eat much else than beans these days. Beans makes you fart."

"Well, wash the beans and try to at least stop gassin' up the air with such smelly ones!"

"Aw, shut the hell up!"

"Boys," Jesse said, dragging off his gloves and then slapping his snow-covered hat against the side of his pants. "How about a little civility?"

"Civil . . . what?"

"You know," Jesse said. "A little good-natured companionship. My name is Jake." He stuck out his hand and shook with the crotchety old trio of codgers. "And while I'm none to happy about this late season snow, I'm still damned glad that I found this barn and your good company."

"What makes you think it's good?" the farter snapped.

"Well," Jesse said, "if it isn't and you can't get that stove started up again, then I guess I'll have no choice but to head outside and make it to the hotel and saloon I passed just up the street."

"Suit yourself," the owner said. "But you owe me four bits and I take only cash in advance."

"As you like," Jesse said, dragging out his wallet and turning his back to the men so they couldn't see how much money he was carrying. He extracted a dollar and turned back to the men. "Here you go. That ought to hold me for the duration of this storm."

The owner took the cash and snapped it like a washrag. He rubbed his old thumb over it and then nodded. "Fair enough, young feller. You can sit with us or take your leave as is your pleasure."

Just then the one man let out a long, rattling fart and a moment later the air was putrid smelling.

"No offense," Jesse said, gathering his bag from the buggy. "But I'll take my leave."

"You'll find your horse rubbed down and fed well come morning," the owner promised. "But the rubbin' down will cost you extra."

"I already paid you extra. A whole damned dollar."

"I guess that might do 'er then," the man said, taking his seat by the stove. "I guess it'll have to."

"What would you give me for that buggy and those matched sorrels?"

The man blinked with surprise. "You'd sell a fine rig like that?"

"For the right price."

"I couldn't give you much."

"Somehow, I knew that you'd say that. Fine. I'll sell them at the next town or the next."

"Let me think on it some. Maybe I can make you a fair offer."

"Better make it good and have the cash in the morning," Jesse warned. "Or I'll be on my way out of this town, and you'll have missed one hell of a deal."

"I'll . . . I'll see what I can do for you," the old man said, looking excited.

Jesse knew that the old man wouldn't be able to pay him what the buggy and sorrels were worth, but he wanted a good saddle horse. If someone was on his trail, he needed to ditch the buggy and sorrels and move faster.

Jesse screwed his hat down tight to keep it from blowing away and headed for the hotel and the saloon. There was nothing in the whole wide world that he wanted more than a bottle of whiskey and a hot bath if they were available. And if not, then any old whore would have to do.

# Chapter 17

Longarm and Alice arrived in the small mountain village of Green Valley during the fierce storm. There was just one hotel, and they were fortunate enough to find a stable and then they hurried to the town's run-down looking hotel.

"Staying long?" the hotel owner asked, unable to keep his eyes off Alice's bosom.

"No," Longarm said sharply. "Just tonight."

The man glanced down at the registry that Longarm had just signed with his name only. "Might have to stay longer if the storm don't let up."

"I hope not."

"The lady your wife?"

"No," Longarm replied. "Not that it's any of your business."

The man was big and jowly with long, greasy black hair. His nose was bent and his hands scarred. He looked like a brawler and boozer and now his face flushed at Longarm's words. "Just trying to be friendly," he said in an offended tone of voice. "You don't have to bite my nose off for it."

"You got a big nose that you ought to keep pointed toward your own business," Longarm told him.

The man pushed up his sleeves to reveal his big, muscular forearms. "Mister, maybe you and your woman should just find another place to wait out the storm."

"You appear to have the only hotel in town."

"That's right. And I got the right to refuse anyone who smart-mouths me a room. Anyone at all."

Longarm's eyes narrowed. "Just try and refuse us a room out of this storm and then we'll see if you can *eat* that damned registration book or if I have to shove it down your throat!"

The hotel owner's eyes widened and he backed up a step, taking Longarm's full measure and deciding that he wanted no part of him. "Mr. Long, you sure ain't a bit friendly."

"It's been a long, hard day," Longarm answered, laying money on the counter. "How much for the room, and it had better be clean."

"Cost you and your woman a dollar." The man glared at Longarm. "Think you can afford that?"

It was all that Longarm could do not to reach across the registration desk and throttle this asshole. But he held his temper in check and left a dollar on the counter. "Give us a key."

The man gave Longarm a room key and then turned away dismissively saying, "I got a small dining room off the kitchen where my Chinese cook serves my guests. But I reckon you and the woman ought to eat somewhere else tonight."

"Is there anywhere else to eat?" Alice asked, laying a steadying hand on Longarm's arm and giving him a frown that said this was not the time or the place to start a fight.

The hotel owner smiled. "Lady, there's a place for you at my table any old day of the week. But not him."

"She asked you a question, you sorry son of a bitch," Longarm growled. "And I think you'd be real smart to give her a civil answer before I come over the top of this counter and whip your arrogant ass."

For a moment, their eyes locked. "There's a café down on the corner."

"Thank you," Alice said, looking exhausted, wet, and be-draggled. "I'd like a hot bath as soon as is humanly possible, if that is available."

The man grinned, showing a gold tooth. "I'll have my Chinaman heat the water and fill the tub. But it'll cost you two bits, lady."

"I'll gladly pay it. And by the way, have you seen a man driving through here in a nice buggy hitched to a matched pair of sorrels?"

"No, can't say that I have. But I don't spend a lot of time staring out at the road watching for passersby."

Longarm turned to Alice. "Might be that someone else saw Jesse come through this place. We'll get you up to our room and you can dry off and take a hot bath while I ask around about him."

"And who would 'him' be?" the hotel man asked.

"He'd be the one driving the buggy pulled by the sorrels," Longarm replied. "What room?"

"Number three and I can escort your woman to the room if you want to go looking for the fella with the buggy."

"No, thanks," Longarm said, not caring for the way the man was staring at Alice and not trusting him even a little. "I'll do it."

"Suit yourself."

The hotel room was small and drab. It wouldn't have had many takers in Denver, but it had a bed, a dresser and basin, and most important of all the roof didn't leak.

"This place isn't very clean," Alice said, shrugging out of her coat and flopping on the bed like a wet and wrung-out dishrag.

"It'll just have to do," Longarm said with a sigh of weary resignation. "With any luck the storm will pass quickly. And we might get lucky and I'll find someone who has seen Jesse. He could even be here in Green Valley."

"I doubt it," she said. "Where else is there that he could stay?"

"Good point," Longarm conceded.

Longarm figured it wouldn't take long to cover the town. There just weren't that many businesses. He had passed an abandoned mine with an immense tailings pile and that told him that Green Valley had once subsisted on gold and silver mining but that the ore had played out. That was pretty typical of mining towns, and Longarm figured that Gold Hill would look about like this town in a few more years. Also, he couldn't understand why it was called Green Valley because there was no valley to speak of. Just tall mountains with a river running through it where there must have once been a long, green meadow. Now, it had all been chewed up and half the shacks he saw on their little homesteads were abandoned.

He went back to the stables where he'd boarded their horses, but the owner hadn't seen Jesse Walker or his buggy. "I keep close to the fire in this cold weather," the man confessed. "And I don't look out the door much. Ain't that many people traveling through here in poor weather. But, if I'd have seen a man in a fine buggy, I'd have remembered."

"Thanks," Longarm said, heading back outside. "Grain those horses heavy this evening and again in the morning. We'll be leaving not long after dawn."

"You will if the weather clears. Might be it won't, mister."

Longarm headed up the street. Most of the faded board storefronts were empty. A few had for-sale or for-rent signs nailed on their locked doors, and Longarm figured that was a lost hope.

At the café on the corner where they would eat this evening, he ducked his head inside to see a heavyset but attractive blond woman sweeping the floor. She had large buttocks and breasts and a nice, wide smile. Longarm didn't mind that her eyes took him in from his boots to his flat-brimmed hat.

"Whatever you are cooking sure smells good," he said, removing the hat and slapping the rain off. "What have you got on the menu for supper?"

"Steaks. Chili. Potatoes, and I've made some pea soup that will warm you up inside. What's your pleasure?" Again, she let her eyes roam to places that might have embarrassed a sensitive man.

"Me and my lady will be back later. What time do you close up?"

"Seven o'clock. Earlier if there's no business. Maybe you ought to sit down and have something to eat now. I am a little starved for conversation and you look like a man that has traveled a bit."

"I have," Longarm admitted. "But I'll come back later with my lady and eat before you close up shop. What I really stopped by for right now is to ask if you have seen a man driving a buggy pulled by sorrels come through this town in the last day or two."

She smiled. "I not only saw him, mister, I fed and then bedded him!" She began to giggle. "Oh, he was nearly as tall and handsome as you and he had a *big* one!"

Longarm did blush a little this time. "Did he say his name?"

"Jake. Just Jake. But then we didn't share much in the way of talk, if you know what I mean."

"I'm pretty sure that I do." Longarm dragged out his marshal's badge and held it up for the woman to see. "Jake isn't his real name . . . or at least I don't think it is. When he was in Denver he called himself Jesse Walker."

"Well," she said, propping the broom up against a scarred little table. "Jake or Jesse, that man knew how to do it to a woman!"

"Fine," Longarm said, wondering if he was going to be able to get her past the story of how they had screwed, probably in the kitchen. "But Jake or Jesse is a killer."

The blond's smile died. "He *killed* someone?"

"Two men in a town called Gold Hill."

"Why, I've been there! I worked for the woman who owns the whorehouse. Her name was . . . uh . . . Bessie. That's right. Good old bossy Bessie. Who'd Jake kill?"

"Two of Gold Hill's leading citizens. Mr. Elmer Wilson and his son Willard."

"Oh my gawd! When I worked for Bessie, Willard Wilson was one of my best customers. He'd come by every Friday afternoon at five o'clock and we'd go for a tumble. He wasn't well hung, but he was a nice, quiet fella. Owned the general store and . . ."

"What's your name?" Longarm asked abruptly.

"Stella. Stella McClure."

"Well, Miss McClure, I'd love to hear about all the men you laid, but I really need to find Jake . . . or Jesse. Did he say where he was headed?"

"No." Stella brushed her fingers through her lustrous blond hair. "Course, I might remember something if I had a little time and maybe . . ."

Longarm knew exactly what Stella was wanting. Him and some extra money. "Here," he said. "Three dollars and you don't even have to raise your skirt. Now where did Jake say he was going?"

"He was going to Nevada."

"You sure that's what he said?"

"Yep. Told me he was a rich man whose family owned a cattle ranch not far from a place called Carson City. That's where he said that he was going."

"And he came by yesterday?"

"That's right. Spent the night at the hotel. Drilled me once in the kitchen and again in his hotel room. He wanted me a third time," Stella said with a wink. "But I had some people here for breakfast, and he seemed in a hurry to leave town."

"What are the names of the towns to the west of us?"

"Well, there is Miner's Junction. Then Deer Flat. Then Horseshoe Bend. And then there is Red Butte and that's starting down the western slope of these damned cold mountains."

"How far is Red Butte?"

"Maybe forty miles. Maybe a little more. Why? Do you think that is where Jake went?"

"I have no idea, but what you've told me is really helpful. Thank you, Stella."

"You said you have a lady traveling with you?"

He paused at the open door. "That's right."

"But you're a United States marshal on a manhunt and you brought a woman along?" She lifted her eyebrows in question. "That doesn't seem right to me if Jake is so dangerous."

"She is Jesse Walker's wife. He married her last week and then tried to strangle her to death a few days later after killing the Wilson men."

Stella swallowed hard. "Maybe Jake was a fooler. I thought he was handsome as hell and a great lover. But it sounds like he had a real mean streak inside of him, huh?"

"You could say that, Stella. And you could say that you got really lucky that he didn't strangle you after he had his pleasure and then rob you of whatever money you have in the till."

"Shit," Stella whispered. "I really was lucky!"

"Damned lucky. See you later for that supper. Hope it's as good as it smells."

"Oh, it is. And, Marshal?"

"Yeah?"

"If you catch up with Jake and take him alive, tell him that Stella wouldn't have been all that easy to kill. I always keep a derringer within reach. Even when I'm humpin' a fella."

"That's a real good thing to do," Longarm said.

"But if you lose the lady, I wouldn't worry about you hurting me any. I can see that you have kind eyes."

Longarm paused and had to ask a question. "Did you look into Jake's eyes and find that they were 'kind'?"

"To tell you the truth, I was looking at other parts of Jake," she said, a grin trying to break through on those ruby-red lips. "If you know what I mean."

"I do," Longarm said, tipping his hat and heading on out the door.

When he got back to the hotel, the owner was missing. Longarm started down to his room and he saw that the door next to another room was cracked just a little. He pushed it open and saw the hotel owner peeking through a little knothole in the wall.

"See something interesting, do you?" Longarm said, fists balling at his sides.

The hotel owner spun around. "I . . . uh . . . no!"

Longarm shoved the big man aside and went over to the knothole. He peeked through it and there was Alice getting ready to climb into a steaming bathtub.

"You sneaky son of a bitch!" Longarm roared, spinning

on his heel and driving an uppercut into the man's gut. "You gawdamn Peeping Tom!"

Longarm went at the man with both fists and a huge rage. His fists landed again and again and when the hotel owner begged for mercy, Longarm grabbed him by the hair and dragged him into the lobby. Still dragging the screaming man by the hair, he hurled him out into the mud of the street and the driving rain.

"If you step foot in this hotel tonight, I'll beat you to within an inch of your life!"

"But it's *my* hotel!" the man sobbed.

"Not tonight it isn't! Now get your degenerate carcass out of my sight, and don't ever let me lay eyes upon you again!"

"I got nowhere else to sleep!"

"You're breaking my heart," Longarm growled as he stomped back into the hotel and out of the storm. He would not tell Alice about this. She had suffered enough humiliation as of late. Adding this sorry Peeping Tom episode to her woes served no good purpose. None at all.

# Chapter 18

Jesse Walker pushed the boozy whore out of his bed and climbed to his feet, feeling dirty and still a little drunk. Bare of feet he stepped across the creaking wooden floor and then peered out of the grimy window of his second-story hotel room.

"Good," he muttered, "blue skies and clear weather."

The whore whose name he had forgotten looked even worse than Jesse felt this morning. Had she looked this awful last night? Probably not. If she had he would not have paid her good money to come to his bed.

"What time is it?" she mumbled.

"It's time for you to get your fat, flabby ass out of my room," he snarled. "Move!"

The whore staggered to her feet and glared at him. "You didn't think my ass was that bad last night when you poked your pole up it twice!"

Jesse wanted to throw up, but instead he grabbed the whore's clothes and threw them at her. "Dress and get out of here."

The whore yanked on her clothes and then stuck out her

hand. "You promised me ten dollars if I'd let you do me in every hole. Now I want my money, buster!"

He balled his fists. "I'll give you something, but it won't be money!"

"You bastard!"

Jesse reached into one of his bags and brought out something, then he shoved it into her hands. "Here, take this, you bitch!"

She stared at the thing in her hands and her eyes grew wide with shock and revulsion. "My gawd, is this what I think it is?"

"Yeah!" he said, grinning. "It's a *scalp* I took not so long ago from someone else dumb enough to piss me off, and you can have it."

"Ahhhh!" she cried, throwing it away.

Jesse punched her in the stomach, and that was a big mistake because she vomited all over his naked lower legs and bare feet. "Jaysus!" he roared as he grabbed the door and threw it open. "You pig!"

She spat and backed up to the door. "You were shot not long ago, and it ain't healing all that well. I hope it gets gangrene and rots all the way to where your heart ought to be!"

"Get out of here before I take your scalp!" he roared.

The woman bolted through the door and he heard her heavy footsteps pounding down the hallway. Jesse smiled and picked up Marvin's scalp. He placed it on the bed and covered it with a blanket. Whoever made the bed fresh would discover it and maybe die of heart failure.

Jesse walked over to the mirror. The bullet that had creased his ribs had left a nasty gash in his side, and it did look to be festering. He would have to find a doctor and get it some medical attention before the wound became a serious problem. But one thing was for sure, he had to keep moving in case the law or a posse was on his trail.

Jesse wiped the pus from his side and winced at the pain. He tore a piece of the bedsheet into strips and used it to bind the wound.

"Okay," he said to himself. "First breakfast, then a doctor, and then I'll get rid of the buggy and get a saddle horse and put some miles between myself and this town."

He studied himself in the mirror one last time before grabbing his bag, and what he saw was pretty shocking. He hadn't shaved in days and there were large, dark circles under his eyes. He looked pale and haggard and decided that he had better find a place in a few days where he could hole up and rest. A place where no one would find him.

Four days and a lot of hard miles later and while nearly at the end of his physical reserves, Jesse rode into Rock Springs, Wyoming. He found the railroad depot and almost toppled from his saddle when he dismounted.

"Mister, are you all right?" a bright-eyed young man who was sweeping the depot asked.

"I've seen better days," Jesse admitted. "Do you happen to know when the next westbound train to Reno comes through here?"

The man extracted a cheap brass pocket watch and consulted it. "Mister," he announced, "the westbound will be through here in about five hours if she's on time. Sometimes she ain't, though. The train can be as much as ten or twelve hours late."

"Five hours," Jessie said more to himself than the young man, "is perfect."

"That horse of yours looks spent," the young man was saying.

"I want to sell him and take the train to Reno," Jesse said. "Where can I sell the animal?"

"Well, sir, there are two stables here in Rock Springs.

There's Abe's and there is Gentry's. Abe's is the bigger one, but he's not as honest as Mr. Gentry. If I had that horse, I'd start at Abe's Stables, get his low offer, then go to Mr. Gentry and see if he'll pay you a few dollars more. But to be honest, that there horse of yours looks like it's on its last legs and I doubt that you'll get more than twenty or twenty-five dollars."

"Yeah," Jesse said, "I figure that's about right. I also need a bath, fresh set of duds, and a shave."

"Mr. Howard has a barber shop and a steady hand with his razor."

"Does he offer hot baths?"

"Yep."

Jesse liked this helpful young man. The kid probably didn't make more than about fifteen dollars a month, but he was smart and amiable, so Jesse dug out a gold coin and used his thumb to flip it in his direction.

"What's this for, mister?"

"It's for your help and for you to take my bag and make sure it doesn't get stolen while I sell my horse and saddle and get a bath, clean clothes, and a shave."

"Why, thank you!" The young man grinned. "Can I take that other little bag and watch over it for you?"

Jesse just shook his head because the "little bag" held almost twenty thousand dollars and a big gold nugget. "But can you take my Winchester and make sure it stays safe until I board the train?"

"I'll put it in the baggage room inside," the kid promised. "Right next to your larger bag. Anything else that I can do to help?"

"No. You've been more than helpful enough. Now point me in the direction of the stables."

The young man gave him directions, which really weren't needed because Rock Springs was just a railroad stop. Jesse climbed wearily back on his horse and rode up to Abe's Stables. The place was a filthy shit hole and there wasn't an animal on the lot that looked as good as the horse he had ridden all the way from Red Butte, so Jesse said to hell with it and rode on down to Gentry's Stables.

"Howdy, mister," a tall, thin man in his thirties called as he pitched hay into a feeder. "That horse you are ridin' looks about done in. Can I put him up for you?"

"I want to sell him," Jesse said. "But not so bad that I'm willing to be skinned."

"Saddle, bridle, and blanket, too?"

"That's right."

"Then you must be going to take the train out of Rock Springs."

"I am."

Gentry nodded and pulled at his beard. "Happens all the time. You from around these parts?"

"Sure," Jesse lied.

Gentry walked all around the horse and then he crouched and ran his hands up and down its legs. He also picked up and inspected all four hooves. "Seems sound enough."

"He is," Jesse said. "Nothing in the world wrong with the animal that some rest and good feed won't fix. I hate to sell him, but I have to get on a train."

"How much money do you want for the horse and what he's carrying?"

Jesse had anticipated the question. "I figure fifty dollars would be about right."

Gentry guffawed and actually slapped at his knee. "Ha! I'm sure you do! But I wouldn't be able to stay in business very much longer if I gave fifty dollars for horses and saddles like yours."

"Then how much will you give me for the animal?"

"How about thirty?"

"No," Jesse bluffed, knowing he'd have to take whatever cash he could get. And he also knew he was being foolish even to dicker, but it just wasn't in his nature to roll over and get taken advantage by anyone, so he had to act as if every dollar he haggled for was important. "How about forty-five?"

"No, sir." Gentry started to turn and walk away.

"Hey," Jesse called.

"What?"

Jesse scowled. "I *need* to sell the horse."

"Go down and see what 'Honest' Abe will offer you, and then you can come back and I'll decide if I can go up on him a little."

"To hell with it," Jesse told the man. "How about thirty-five dollars?"

Gentry looked at the animal a long time, then he opened his mouth and checked his teeth. "This horse is only about six or seven years old. I'll give you thirty-five for him and the saddle."

"Deal," Jesse said, knowing that the man could fatten up the gelding and resell him at a tidy profit. "So long as you're paying in cash."

Gentry laughed. "Well, I sure didn't think you wanted payment in sacks of oats!"

They both laughed. Gentry took the animal and Jesse pocketed his cash, then he headed up the street toward a general store where he would buy himself a complete outfit of new clothes and a hat. His clothes and hat were a muddied and rumpled mess, and there wasn't time to have them cleaned.

He carried his new duds over to the barber shop. Two hours later and after a hearty breakfast he came out of the barber shop looking like a new man. He next made a quick stop at a doctor's office and had his wound cleaned and disinfected.

"You've been shot, haven't you?" the doctor asked, examining the wound with a critical eye.

Jesse decided that there was no point in lying. "That's right."

"And you got shot about a week ago, I'd say from the looks of this."

"Doc, is it going to heal all right?" Jessie asked.

"It should have been stitched up," the doctor, an older man with a little white goatee, muttered. "Stitched up and taken care of. But then you know that, don't you?"

"Doc, can you give me a little medicine so it heals up right?"

"I can do that," the doctor said. "And I'll bandage it up and give you some clean fresh bandaging so that you don't have to resort to using strips of bedsheets."

"Much obliged."

The doctor finished taking care of and bandaging the wound. "Did you kill him?"

"Who?"

"The man that shot you?"

"Doc, you ask way too many damned questions," Jesse warned. "And you'd do well to stick to doctorin'."

"I guess that's good advice. This and the bandages and medicine I'll give you to take away will cost you twenty-five dollars."

Jesse scowled. "That's pretty damned high."

"Not as high as you'd have paid if you'd have waited any longer to have a *real* doctor attend to that wound. Another day and the infection would have gotten into your blood, and you would have been on your back with a fever and maybe on your way to the morgue."

"Are you serious, Doc?"

"As serious as gangrene. Didn't you smell yourself?"

"I did," Jesse admitted. "But I just thought it was infected."

"Oh, it was! Well infected. You really should rest up for a few days and take things real easy. If a man my age had a wound that had been neglected like that, it would most likely have been fatal."

Jesse gulped. "I'll take care of it. And I'll give you an extra ten dollars for a little extra bandaging and medicine."

"That would be smart, sir. Very smart indeed."

Five hours and twenty minutes later the train pulled into the little depot to take on coal and water. By then Jesse Walker had his ticket for Reno and a bottle of whiskey in the satchel resting next to all his cash and the gold nugget.

"This train stay here for very long?" he asked the porter.

"About an hour. You in a hurry, sir?"

"I just want to get to Nevada," he said wearily. "I just want to be on my way."

"We'll be in Ogden before you know it," the porter promised. "This time of year we keep pretty much on schedule and the Paiutes out in the desert don't bother us much anymore."

"But they used to?"

"Oh, yes. They used to pile rocks and trees and anything else they could find across the tracks. They hated the 'Iron Horse,' but we just rolled right on through their lands and they finally gave up trying to stop us."

"I expect they did give up," Jesse said. "Bunch of desert rats, if you ask me. Nothing but lizard and bug eaters."

"I'll get you a blanket and some pillows. You look like you could use some overdue sleep. Want me to take those bags and . . ."

"Thanks, but no, thanks. I'll just keep them right here beside me all the way to Reno."

"Whatever suits you," the porter said with a smile.

When he was alone with only his thoughts, Jesse dragged out his bottle of whiskey and took a long, badly needed pull as he stared out the window. He wondered if Marshal Long and a posse were closing in on him or if he'd lost them in the mountains. It had rained in the last few days and he had switched to a horse, but anyone on his trail would have found the buggy that he'd sold and figured out what he was up to next. What they wouldn't know was exactly how he was going to get to Nevada.

Most likely, though, they'd figure he had ridden straight into Utah and across the great desert. They weren't likely to guess that he'd made an abrupt turn of direction to the north and ridden all the way to Rock Springs, Wyoming.

Maybe they were even now riding into the deserts of Utah and Nevada. And best of all, maybe they were all going to get scalped by the Paiutes.

He remembered the look of horror that had been on the whore's face when he'd thrown her that fresh scalp. And then, Jesse closed his eyes and chuckled as he took another deep pull on his bottle.

# Chapter 19

Longarm and Alice reined in their horses and stared at a vista stretching for hundreds of miles. "Well," Longarm said, standing up in his stirrups, "today we have a big decision to make."

"What is that?"

Longarm pointed down at the great valley and the river below. "That's the Green River and those far snow-capped peaks are the Uinta Mountains. So, assuming that Jesse is really heading for Carson City, we need to decide if we should push on across the mountains straight toward Salt Lake City, or if we should cut north and follow the Green River all the way up to the transcontinental railroad."

"Why would we go to the railroad?" Alice asked.

"Lots of reasons. First thing is we could ride the train across the deserts of Utah and northern Nevada to Reno."

"But what if Jesse is just up ahead someplace?" Alice asked.

"I don't think he wants to cross the high mountains of Utah or the Great Basin deserts any more than I do," Longarm told her. "There's a couple hundred miles of badlands as the crow flies between us and Carson City. The Paiutes are always looking for easy pickings, and the crossing is hard and dangerous. If we go north and catch the railroad at Rock Springs, we'll be in Reno a whole lot faster and at considerably less hardship."

"Then that's what we should do," Alice said.

"I agree. And since we've lost Jesse's trail several days ago, we might find someone in Rock Springs who remembers him buying a ticket for Reno. I think that is a fair possibility."

Alice sighed. "If we catch the westbound transcontinental, will it go through Salt Lake City?"

"No. It goes through Ogden and stays north of Salt Lake City."

"But what if *that's* where Jesse went?"

It was a good question, and Longarm gave it a fair amount of thought before he answered. "Salt Lake City is the headquarters for the Mormons, and your husband doesn't strike me as a man who would either fit in or get along well with church-minded people."

"That's true," Alice conceded.

"Then we'll ride down to the Green River and follow it north until we hit the tracks then follow it west into Rock Springs," Longarm said, giving his tired horse a bump with his heels.

Alice followed and they made it down to the Green River that night and camped beside the strong-flowing river. Longarm and Alice ate the last of their meager food supply and finally rolled into their blankets to gaze up at the cold stars.

"Where does the Green River go?" she asked.

"It joins the Colorado and flows all the way through the Arizona Territory. It cuts through the Grand Canyon and runs down to the Gulf of Mexico," Longarm told her. "Must be a thousand miles. I don't know. But it's a hell of a long way."

"Have you ever been down there?"

"To the Gulf of Mexico?"

"Yes."

"I have," Longarm said. "It's different from anything you've ever seen, but it's hot and dry country getting there and sometimes it's hard to find fresh water if you stray from the Colorado River. The Yuma Territorial Prison is one of the worst hellholes in the entire Southwest. I've been there and the prisoners really suffer in the summer heat. Once a week they chain 'em all together and march them down to the Colorado River to bathe and just to cool off . . . those prisoners that have earned that right with their good behavior. Those that have not been on good behavior have to stay in their cells and suffer."

"I'll bet getting into the river is quite an incentive to behave," Alice said thoughtfully.

"It sure is," Longarm agreed. "A lot of prisoners die of the heat and plenty try to escape. But they have towers and guards with rifles, and they know that the only hope a prisoner has of getting out of that country is by sticking to the river. So most are caught right away. I've seen a lot of prisons in my time, Alice, but the Yuma Territorial Prison is the worst of them all."

"Custis, you've been to a lot more places than I have," Alice said, turning to him.

"Maybe so, but there are plenty of them I'd rather *not* have seen," Longarm admitted. "There is some hot, dry, and ugly country between us and the gulf. It's easy country to get killed in and I wouldn't want to risk the crossing with you at my side."

She touched his face. "I'll go anywhere to find Jesse and bring him to justice!"

"You've held up real well so far, Alice. You're not only strong and brave, you're pretty tough."

"Thank you." She slipped under his blanket and her hand found his thigh. "I'm also a woman who needs attention on cold and starry nights."

"Is that what you want now?"

"Uh-huh."

"I can take care of that," he told her.

"I know you can." She began to undo her buttons. "So do it."

A few minutes later, Longarm was making love to Alice and with the starry sky above and the crackling fire beside them it was real nice and easy. He didn't take her roughly, but instead gently and he stretched things out for a long, long time. Finally, however, Alice climbed on top and rode him hard until they were both well satisfied and shaking with the aftershocks of their intense pleasure.

"That was nice," she said, climbing off and lying down beside him. "Really nice."

"I liked it, too."

"We ought to do it more often," she told him. "Just in case."

"In case what?"

"In case Jesse ambushes and kills us."

Longarm stared up at the heavens. There was almost a full moon out tonight, and the sound of the rushing river filled his ears. "Alice," he said, "I think you've just hit upon a real good idea because Jesse could be waiting for just the right place to draw a rifle's bead on me. This country has a million places where a man could lay an almost perfect ambush. And if he did, our only chance of survival would be if the ambusher missed his first shot and we had time to take cover."

"Jesse said he was a good rifle shot."

"I imagine that he is," Longarm said. "Ever since he traded those sorrels and that rented buggy in for a saddle horse, I've been trying to watch for ambush places hoping I'd outguess the man. But he seems to have just wanted to keep on the move."

"Let's hope that we can find him at the family's big cattle ranch," Alice said.

"Yeah," Longarm agreed. "If Jesse even has one."

"I think that he does," Alice told him after a long pause. "It was all that Jesse talked about when we were alone." She poked him in the side. "When we talked, that is."

Longarm knew what she meant, and although he was much too much of a gentleman to broach the subject, he was pretty sure that Jesse had been a passionate and enthusiastic lover.

"You're better than Jesse," she said, as if reading his mind. "Jesse was a passionate and ardent lover, but he was rough and often selfish. Not you, though."

"Maybe you'd like doing it with me better if I was rougher," Longarm said, only half teasing.

"No," she told him. "Well, not very often anyway."

"I'll keep that in mind," he promised as he closed his eyes and drifted off to sleep.

# Chapter 20

Jesse Walker jumped down from the train even before it came to a complete stop at the Reno depot. He took a deep breath of clean Nevada air and headed directly for a stage-coach outfit that he knew ran twice daily to Carson City via the Comstock Lode.

"Afternoon," he said, coming to rest at the counter. "I'd like a one-way ticket to Carson City."

"I'm afraid that the coach is filled for this afternoon," the ticket agent said. "But I can book you for tomorrow morning."

"This afternoon's coach is booked solid?"

"Yes, sir."

"But surely it will carry one more passenger. I need to get to Carson City tonight."

"I'm really sorry, but as you may know, it's a steep and winding road up to Virginia City. I'm sure you wouldn't want our fine team of horses to be hurt pulling an overloaded coach."

Jesse's smile turned sour. "I don't give a damn about your horses! I want to leave on the next coach."

"Well," the agent said, his posture stiffening. "I just told you we are sold out, and you'll have to return tomorrow. See those people out there on the platform?"

"I see 'em."

"They are the eight that are waiting for the team and coach, which should be here any minute. Now, would you like to buy a ticket for tomorrow or not?"

"If one of those eight passengers changed his mind about going on this run, then I would be his replacement?"

"Sure," the agent said. "But . . ."

"How much for a ticket?"

"Five dollars."

Jesse bought a ticket. The agent said, "The stage leaves at ten o'clock sharp tomorrow morning. We allow one bag with the ticket. If you have two bags it costs an extra dollar and they can't weigh over thirty pounds each."

"Fine," Jesse said, paying the man and scooping up his ticket. He walked outside, glaring at the eight passengers. One of them, a tall, angular fellow in his fifties dressed in a white shirt and black collar and wearing a derby hat, was obviously a low-stakes gambler.

Jesse walked over to the man, who had gotten up and was standing alone and watching for the stagecoach. "Mister, I'll give you five dollars if you take the stagecoach tomorrow and give me your seat on this run. I need to get to Carson City, and I'm in a hurry."

The gambler's cheeks were sunken and his complexion gray. He looked like a tubercular. Jesse kept his distance lest the diseased man cough.

He looked Jesse up and down with a cool appraisal and then said, "You will pay me *twenty* dollars and I'll give you my seat."

The gambler smiled without warmth and extracted a cheap cigar from his coat pocket, lighting it and blowing a smoke ring in Jesse's direction.

"Twenty dollars, huh?" Jesse's eyes tightened at the corners. "You want me to pay you twenty dollars for a five-dollar ticket?"

"That's right," the man said coolly, "I can read men's minds, and you look downright desperate. I don't care about your needs or business, but it will cost you twenty dollars for my ticket in exchange for your own on tomorrow morning's stage."

"All right," Jesse said, reaching into his coat and dragging out his wallet. "Deal."

The man chuckled at his victory. He gave Jesse his ticket and extended his bony hand. "I sure guessed right about you being desperate, didn't I, young man?"

"You did in one respect, but not in another," Jesse said, putting his wallet away without giving the man money.

"What . . ."

"Sorry," Jesse said, "but I decided to not only keep my own ticket but take yours for free."

The gambler's ravaged face tightened with rage and his hand shot under his coat for what Jesse knew would be either a knife or a derringer. Jesse stepped in close and drove a powerful right uppercut into the tubercular's stomach, causing the thin man to gasp and bend over in agony. Then Jesse stepped back and kicked upward, his toe connecting with the gambler's jaw. The man's head snapped back and he crashed to the platform unconscious.

"Hey!" the stagecoach agent who had sold Jesse a ticket shouted as he came running outside. "You can't do that to one of our passengers!"

"I just did," Jesse told him as everyone stared. "And if you don't want the same, you'll get back into that office and keep your gawdamn mouth shut!"

The ticket agent skidded to a halt, and his eyes darted from Jesse down to the unconscious gambler. "You *really* hurt him," the agent said, shaking his head with worry. "He's obviously not a well man."

"I can see that, but it's not my problem nor should it be yours unless you want to make a lot of trouble for yourself," Jesse said. "Ah, here comes my stagecoach right now!"

Jesse bulled his way onto the coach ahead of two women and the other men. He smiled and began to hum a tune. He was almost home, and he sure liked the scent of desert sage.

He watched the ticket agent kneel beside the unconscious gambler. The man was frantically gesturing for help and two teenagers came running.

"We need to get him inside and get a doctor!" Jesse heard the agent shout.

"What kind of a man are you!" one of the women who had boarded the stagecoach choked. "You might have killed that poor, unwell gentleman!"

"I doubt that very much," Jesse said. "He's a lunger and he should never have been allowed to ride with healthy people like ourselves."

"But you really hurt him!"

"Ma'am, if you don't shut up, I'll slap the shit out of you."

"You can't talk to a lady like that!" an angry passenger protested with outrage.

Jesse yanked out his pistol, cocked the hammer, and said, "Get off this coach or get shot."

The man couldn't get out of the coach fast enough and three others went with him including the woman who had scolded Jesse. "Lots of room to stretch now and enjoy the ride," he said to the remaining passengers. "But you don't have to thank me for your newfound comfort."

They turned their heads away from him and stared outside. Jesse leaned over to the window and shouted, "Driver, get this son of a bitch rolling, or I'll come up there and do it myself!"

The stagecoach jolted forward and Jesse smiled as he re-holstered his gun. "Some people," he said, "just don't seem to get the message unless you are firm with them. Wouldn't you agree?"

No one said a word and they avoided his eyes. Jesse knew they were all afraid and that he would not hear any sass from any of them on his journey to Carson City.

# Chapter 21

Late the next afternoon, Jesse rode out of Carson City on a lively and beautiful liver-chestnut–colored mare that caught the eye of everyone in the main street. The mare and the nice saddle he'd bought for his going-home family reunion cost him $125, which was a fortune. What the hell, he had a fortune in cash and old Elmer Wilson's prized gold nugget.

His ranch was south of town, and it had been in his family since he was a boy. Like every ranch, it had seen its share of good times and bad, and given the prolonged drought that this part of the country was in, it was a wonder that his family had even been able to hold on to it the past six or seven years. Even now as he rode south he saw very few of his family's cattle, and those that he did see were in wretched physical condition. They were so thin that their ribs could be counted, just like with himself. But sooner or later the drought would break in western Nevada, and as for his own poor physical condition, he would fatten up like he always did when he was at home and at peace with the world.

He tried not to remember the day that he had fought with his kid brother and his father. Hard words had been exchanged and all because Jesse had gambled away some of the cookie jar money and then gotten drunk and arrested in town. His father had bailed him out of jail, but he'd hurt two men badly and there were going to be lawsuits against him for assault and battery, plus the medical costs of sewing up the men he'd beaten. But those two had asked for a fight, and he'd just made sure that they'd gotten what they deserved. Sure, he shouldn't have beaten them nearly unconscious and then broke a whiskey bottle and taken it to their faces, but he'd bet they never wanted a piece of him again, by gawd!

Jesse laughed at the memory. That would teach them to mess with a Walker man!

When he arrived late that afternoon he felt like he had at last come home from something akin to being at war. He'd been gone nearly five years, traveling all over the place, robbing people and a couple of times even banks. He'd carried his own weight in those hard years and then he'd met Alice, and she in turn had connected him with her grandfather, the rich old Mr. Wilson. The dead old Mr. Wilson, now. Well, it had been one hell of a profitable experience, and he'd kept his neck from getting stretched, and now he was coming home a wealthy man. Wait until his folks and his kid brother saw the color of his money. My, they'd be impressed!

The Walker ranch house wasn't big, just a single-story rambling log affair whose labyrinth of rooms had been added to over the years as money permitted. Jesse's mother had died eight years earlier while trying to deliver her first daughter, and nothing had been right with the family ever since. After his mother's sad passing, Pa had hired a succession of maids and cooks, but the old man was so demanding and irascible that sooner or later he drove them all away. He'd raped one young housemaid, and she'd immediately filed charges in Carson City, but the charges couldn't be proven and when Pa had given the girl fifty dollars, she'd just disappeared.

"Well," Jesse said to himself as he studied the family's ranch house, "all that is about to change. I'm coming home with over nineteen thousand dollars and a gold nugget almost as big as a robin's egg. Now I guess that I'll finally get a little respect from my pa and kid brother."

As Jesse neared the yard a pair of big dogs came charging out from under the porch. His high-strung mare snorted with fear and started crow-hopping, and Jesse had his hands full trying to settle the mare and avoid getting bucked off while shouting at the dogs to shut up and back off. When the liver-chestnut mare whirled and bucked, Jesse went flying. He struck the ground hard and felt a sharp pain lance through his side where the old bullet wound was still healing.

"Damn!" Jesse was so enraged that he rolled to his knees, drew his gun, and shot both of the damned ranch dogs until his gun was empty and the mongrels were twisting and whining around in their own blood.

"Hey!" Jesse's father shouted, coming out of the house with a shotgun clenched in his fists. "Gawdamn you, Jesse! Those were good watchdogs, and I liked 'em!"

Jesse climbed to his feet and holstered his empty gun. He heard the sound of pounding hooves and whirled around to see his beautiful mare galloping off. He swore, knowing it was headed back to Carson City and the livery where he'd bought the animal.

"Damnit, Pa! Those dogs almost got me killed!"

"They were brothers and good watchdogs. I use 'em to hunt coyotes and cougars, and now you've shot the shit outta 'em and they're dying!"

The old man had aged a lot in the hard years during Jesse's departure, and now he looked weary and unwell. Elias Walker shuffled over to the pair of dying dogs, said a few comforting words, and then blasted them both to put them out of their terrible misery.

"Son of a bitch!" his father shouted in anger. "Jesse, you ain't here one minute and you've already made trouble."

"Pa, didn't you see those dogs coming at me and the mare? Don't you see my horse running back toward Carson City, and don't you even give a damn that I got dumped in my own ranch yard and hurt?"

"You're standin'," old Elias Walker snapped. "And as for what happened you shouldn't have allowed yourself to be thrown! I thought you was raised to ride a helluva lot better'n that!"

Jesse shook his head in exasperation. He and his old man had never gotten along, and he could see that, money or not, that wasn't going to change. "You don't look so good, Pa."

"You don't, either," the old man shot back. "You look thin enough to take a bath in the barrel of my shotgun."

"Aw, shit," Jesse said, "I'm not *that* thin."

"Yes, you are," the old man insisted. "From where I'm standing it appears that you're just moving around to save funeral expenses."

Jesse shook his head and decided to change the subject. "How is my kid brother? Is Dan still doing well and walking the straight and narrow road? Did he marry Cecilia Allen yet?"

"No," Elias said, "he never married Cecilia. She found a man with money and tossed your brother aside as if he was a piece of garbage. It nearly broke Dan's heart."

Jesse snorted with disgust. "Dan can do a lot better than Cecilia. I never told him, but I screwed her plenty, and she wasn't much good in bed."

"Jesus," Elias said, "don't ever tell your brother what you was doing!"

"What difference would it make now?"

Elias reloaded his big double-barreled shotgun. "It shouldn't make any difference, but I think he's still half in love with the girl. Last I heard, she and her husband had moved to San Francisco."

"Good riddance to Cecilia." Jesse glanced toward the quiet ranch house. "Where is Dan?"

"Gone to the Comstock Lode to work."

"He's a hard-rock miner?"

"That's right," Elias said. "We lost the ranch, and there was no work here and we had no money. They got a good miner's union up in Virginia City and Dan is making sixty dollars a month. He visits now and then and brings me vittles and some spending cash. He's a good son, not like some I can think of."

Jesse was stung by the old man's thinly veiled message but chose to ignore it and said, "What do you mean that you 'lost the ranch'? We're standing on it, aren't we?"

"We are but now it's owned by some fella up in Virginia City that is a successful lawyer and has a lot of money. Name is Gardner . . . Mr. Thomas T. Gardner. He bought my ranch on the auction block about four months ago."

His father sighed. "Mr. Gardner bought the whole shebang for just over three thousand dollars. And even that money all went to pay off the local merchants that had given us credit for table food and what few livestock we tried to keep from starving during the drought and hard winters."

Jesse staggered at this news. "Pa, are you telling me that you sold our house, the land, even the livestock? *Everything?*"

Elias looked away and blinked. "I didn't really sell it, Jesse. The bank had a note, and they're the ones that sold it out from under me. Sold everything but the clothes on my back and a few old saddle horses that weren't worth anything. I'm just tending the place now."

"You're a *caretaker*?" Jesse asked, the word nearly choking him because it had such a bitter sound.

"I am," Elias shamefully confessed. "Mr. Gardner pays me thirty dollars a month to protect the house and the barn from vandals. As soon as he sells the ranch for a profit, I'll be thrown off the land."

"No, by gawd, you won't!" Jesse vowed. "Because I'm going to buy it back for us."

The old man was so wrapped in his misery that he was not listening. "The Walker family is out of the ranching business, Jesse. Next week I'm gonna have your ma and sister exhumed and their bodies buried in the Carson City Cemetery. When the ranch sells and I'm kicked off, I'll move to town and try to find a job that will feed me."

"The hell you say!" Jesse stormed. "We're a *ranching* family and I'm going to buy this place back! Nobody is taking it from us! Not now and not ever!"

Elias finally heard his youngest son. "You always did have trouble dealing with the truth, Jesse. Don't matter. Maybe Dan can help you get a job in the mines and sign you up with the miner's union."

Jesse grabbed the old man and shook him by his bony shoulders. "You aren't listening to me, Pa! You *never* listened to me but by gawd you are going to listen to me now! I'm going to buy this ranch back and then I'm going to restock it with as many cattle as the grass will stand. And we're going to be prosperous again. The Walker brand meant something in this part of the country when I was growing up here, and it will regain the respect it has lost!"

Elias looked up into his son's burning eyes. "How are you going to do that, Jesse? How are you going to get the ranch back for us?"

Jesse released his father and reached inside of his coat pocket. He'd been wise to keep the money on his person since leaving Gold Hill instead of in his saddlebags, which were now heading back to town. He tore out his wallet and yanked out a thick stack of bills.

"Look here, Pa! Look at all the money I've got. These are all fifty- and one-hundred-dollar bills. I have about nineteen thousand dollars in my hand, and I'm going to use it to buy back this ranch and restock it with purebred beef cattle and good cow horses that we can breed, raise, break, and sell at a profit."

Elias Walker stared at the money unable to tear his eyes from it. Finally, he reached out and laid his hands on the cash. "Was it stolen or tainted by innocent blood?"

"Hell no!"

"Then where . . ."

"Gambling," Jesse lied. "You remember how I always loved to gamble."

"Yeah, I do," Elias said. "But you weren't good at it. You'd lose more often than win, and when you lost you'd take revenge."

"Well . . . that was then and this is now," Jesse assured the old man. "So what we are going to do is to go up to Virginia City tomorrow, find Mr. Thomas T. Gardner, who took advantage of our hard times, and make him sell it back to us at no profit."

Elias swallowed hard. "You reckon he might do that?"

Jesse Walker nodded and began punching shells into his revolver with a vengeance. "I'm just going to make that rich Mr. Gardner the kind of offer that . . . one way or another . . . he would be insane to refuse."

Tears spilled out of the old eyes, and Elias covered his sun-ravaged face with his trembling hands.

Jesse wasn't often moved by sympathy, but he felt a knot in his throat getting big when he said, "Don't cry, Pa. I'm sorry that I didn't come back sooner, but I'm home now and I've got all the money we'll need to start out bigger and better than we ever were in the past."

"So long as it ain't *blood* money, Jesse. If it's blood money, no good will come of it. No good at all."

"Money is money, Pa, and it all spends just the same. You'll see. Tomorrow we'll go to Virginia City and set everything to rights. We'll find my brother and let Dan know that no Walker man needs to swing a pick down in some gawdamn hard-rock mine! You'll see, Pa!"

Elias Walker dipped his chin. "I just can't believe that you came home alive . . . much less with so much money. You done real, real good, Jesse. I never thought you'd do anything but wind up hanging from a tree, but I can see now that I was wrong."

"You were wrong, Pa."

"Well, I'm man enough to admit the fact, Jesse. Yes, sir! I'm man enough to see that I judged you unfairly, and I'm going to make up for that."

Jesse finished reloading. "You got any food or whiskey in the house?"

"A little of both."

"Don't suppose you got a maid like the one you screwed and who raised such a fuss."

The old man cackled. "No, but I sure would like to have 'er back!"

They laughed together and walked back into the house. Jesse was feeling real good about things now, and he was damn glad he had come all the way back home.

# Chapter 22

Longarm and Alice rode into Rock Springs in the southwest corner of the Wyoming Territory. The town had a hard look to it, and there weren't a lot of smiles on the faces of the people they saw.

"I can't say that I like this country that much," Longarm admitted as they tied their horses up in front of the railroad depot. We're in what is called the Bridger Basin, named after the famous mountain man Jim Bridger."

Alice was so stiff and sore from the long miles of riding that she had to be helped out of her saddle. "I thought mountain men trapped beaver in the pines."

"They trapped beaver, all right. But they'd trap 'em in rivers and streams that flowed through hard, dry country like we're in now. There is this stinking desert river that wanders across the Nevada Territory called the Humboldt. In the early days, it was trapped out of beaver and in the later days it's the path that the pioneers followed getting across the desert."

"Thanks for the history lesson, Custis, but are you aware that people are staring at us?"

"They're not staring at me. They are starting at *you*," Longarm said with amusement.

"Why, because they never saw such a weary and be-draggled woman?"

"Because they don't see many women at all except for the dance hall girls and whores," Longarm told her. "Rock Springs is a hardscrabble railroad town. I suppose there are some big ranches that ship cattle out of here because I saw the stockyards, but most of the town's economy relies on the railroad. If the railroad went away, so would Rock Springs."

"What are we going to do now?" she asked.

"We'll tie the horses up, and you sit and rest easy while I go into the depot and see if anyone has recognized Jesse."

He spotted a teenager sweeping the depot floor. "Hey, got a minute!"

The kid stopped sweeping. "Can I help you, sir?"

"I hope so," Longarm replied. "I'm looking for a man that might have boarded a train for Nevada out of here in the last couple of days."

"There's a lot of men that do."

"But this one was tall like myself, and he'd have been riding a played-out horse. He'd have had a satchel or two and he was wearing good clothes, but they'd have been badly soiled."

"Was he headed for Reno?" the kid asked.

"That's right. Did you see him?"

"Who's asking?"

Longarm showed the kid his federal officer's badge. "What's your name?"

"Martin Crawley."

"Well, Martin, do you see that woman I rode in with that is sitting over there with our horses?"

"Sure." He blushed. "Everybody in town has seen her, I reckon."

"Well, the man that you saw robbed and killed her grandfather and uncle and then he tried to strangle that pretty young lady to death."

Martin's eyes widened. "He did?"

"Yep. And I'm after him before he kills any more good people. So tell me all that you can about him."

Martin Crawley looked rattled, and he had to swallow a few times before saying, "He was nice to me. The gentleman asked where he could sell his horse and saddle and I told him that Abe's Stables would probably give him the fairest price."

"And did he sell his outfit?"

"He did and then he got on the westbound and left for Reno two days ago."

"Damn," Longarm swore. "I was hoping that he was too worn out to travel right away and would hole up here in Rock Springs."

"No, sir!" Martin said. "That man was in a hurry to leave. And now I guess I can figure out why."

Longarm scowled. "When does the next train depart for Reno?"

The young man pulled out his cheap brass watch. "You're in luck, Marshal. Next train will be here in exactly sixty-five minutes . . . if she's runnin' on time."

"Sixty-five minutes is cutting it close," Longarm said. "I need to buy two tickets to Reno and sell these horses and saddles."

"I can buy your tickets while you go over to Abe's. Just tell him that Martin sent you and to give you a fair deal or I won't send him any more customers." The kid walked over to their horses, tipping his hat to Alice and studying the animals and saddles.

"You probably paid a lot more for 'em than you'll get trying to sell 'em to Abe in a hurry, but you ought to get sixty dollars."

Longarm frowned. "For the horses, saddles, bridles, blankets, and everything?"

"Horses are real cheap in Wyoming," the young man said with a shrug of his broad shoulders. "And those saddles aren't worth much. Any self-respecting cowboy wouldn't have use for either one of 'em."

"All right," Longarm said. "We'll let Abe skin us on the deal and then hurry back and board the train."

"Don't take too much time," the kid warned. "It doesn't happen very often but the train has been known to arrive and then leave a few minutes early."

"We'll be here," Longarm vowed.

Their experience at Abe's Stables went about as expected. Abe wanted to give them practically nothing for the animals because he sensed that they had a train to catch and there was no chance to dicker. But at last they settled on sixty dollars and hurried toward the train depot.

"We could have got twice that much for them in Denver," Alice said as he helped her up the street.

"I know, but Abe knew that he had us over a barrel. Let's just get on the train and then we can rest, eat, and relax."

"Will they have a bath available?"

Longarm nodded. "They sure will, and you'll have to arm wrestle me to see who gets in it first."

"Maybe it's big enough that we could get in it together," Alice said, summoning up a smile.

"Now wouldn't that cause tongues to wag," Longarm said. "The whole train would hear about it and since it's pretty much given that young Martin Crawley told the conductor that I'm a federal marshal it would really be a scandal."

"I'm glad that you didn't tell Martin that Jesse was my husband."

"*Is* your husband, Alice. The wedding ceremony was legal."

She stiffened for a moment and then said with great firmness, "Jesse is already a dead man in my mind. So you see, in my mind he only *was* my husband."

"I understand," Longarm said, not wanting to debate the issue.

"All aboard!" the conductor shouted. "All aboard!"

"How far does this train go?" Alice asked.

"All the way to Sacramento."

"And how far is that from San Francisco?"

"Less than a day on a stage line."

"I'd like to go to San Francisco with you when this ordeal is over," she said. "I always wanted to see that city and the Pacific Ocean. We could swim in it and have fun. Put this terrible manhunt behind us and wash it clean away with ocean water."

"We'll see," Longarm told her. "But first there is that little matter of Jesse Walker, who I'm sure is not going to surrender without a fight."

"Jesse will go down with his gun blazing. You'd better know that for a fact."

"I'd already figured that out."

"He'll be trying to kill you," Alice said, "figuring you are the one most likely to kill him first. But he'll be wrong."

Longarm glanced sideways at her as they rushed across the board platform to the train. "What does that mean?"

"It means he won't be looking at me when I shoot him on sight."

Longarm realized that he was going to have to have a heart-to-heart talk with Alice or she was going to get herself killed or tossed in prison. And he didn't want that. Actually, he really did like the idea of walking side by side with Alice on the sandy beaches of the blue Pacific.

# Chapter 23

Jesse hitched up an old buckboard to a sorry, sway-backed old bay gelding, and they headed for Virginia City to find Dan Walker and the man that had bought their ranch at auction for a mere three thousand dollars.

Carson City was located at the base of the Sierra Nevada Mountains. Up a very long and steep mountain grade you could get to Lake Tahoe, and that's where you found tall pines and a lot of timber mills. It snowed something fierce at Lake Tahoe, but not nearly so bad in the Carson Valley. No, down here at the base of the Sierras the wind howled, and what you had was mostly sagebrush and rock with a few nice little ranches situated along the Carson River and in a little Mormon community called Genoa.

Carson City was the territorial capital of Nevada and so there was a governor's mansion, a capitol building, and a bunch of other government offices. But all in all it was a very quiet town that had always been overshadowed by Virginia City, the rip-roaring "Queen of the Comstock" and source of millions of dollars in gold and silver from the deep mines.

"Do you know what mine Dan is working for?" Jesse asked.

"I believe he said it was the Consolidated Mine . . . or maybe it was the Chollar."

"We'll find him, but I'm more interested in locating this Gardner fella and getting our ranch bought back."

"I don't know where to find the man."

Jesse whipped the sorry gelding on the rump to make it move faster. "This sure is a worthless horse we got hitched to this even more worthless wagon."

"They took all my good things," Elias said bitterly. "Even took my only good milk cow and the two pigs I was fattening."

"Gardner took 'em?"

"That's right. He was there at the auction, and since there were no other bidders he paid the minimum price set by the bank. He got everything that was worth anything. That's why we don't have much furniture in the house. No tools, and they'd have taken this old horse and wagon if they thought that they could have made money on 'em."

"Pa, first thing I'm going to do is have a long, serious talk to this Thomas T. Gardner fella and make him see the injustice that he has done to our respected ranching family."

"Now, Jesse. You shouldn't be too hard on the man. He gave me fifty dollars out of his pocket and explained that, if he hadn't bought the ranch and all our stuff, someone else would have done it for even less money. I don't rightly hold it against Mr. Gardner."

"Well, I sure as hell do," Jesse grated as they passed through Carson City going east toward the road that would climb up to Sun Mountain and the Comstock Lode.

It was late that day when their horse just gave out up on the steep grade that roughly followed the Virginia & Truckee Railroad that connected Virginia City with Carson City.

They had struggled upward through Devil's Gate and then Silver City, but their horse just couldn't make it over the steep and narrow divide that separated Silver City and Virginia City. The old animal just sighed and fell over in its harness right in the middle of the busy road.

"Quit whippin' him!" Elias shouted. "Gawdamn you, Jesse, you always were hell on animals and women. Can't you see that he's down and he ain't gettin' up unless we unhitch him from this wagon!"

"I'll shoot the sorry son of a bitch!" Jesse screamed as huge ore wagons started to back up on the divide due to their blocking of it. "I'll just shoot him on the spot!"

"No, you won't!" a bearded and angry-looking teamster shouted as he hauled up on his lines and tied down the break. "Can't you see that poor horse done its best!"

"Well, it wasn't good enough, and I'll kill him!"

"You do that," another teamster shouted, jumping into the argument, "and every one of us teamsters will whip your ass into a bloody pulp!"

"Then what the hell are we supposed to do!" Jesse railed.

"Get off your lazy butts, cut the poor old horse free, and we'll help you push that piece of shit wagon off the side of the road. Then you and that old man walk your worthless asses up over the divide into Virginia City!"

Jesse started to go red with fury, but his father grabbed his arm and hissed, "Damnit, Jesse, if you don't do what they're tellin' ya to do, we're going to be landin' in a hornet's nest! You can't take on all these big fellas!"

"Watch me, Pa. Just watch me!"

But Elias managed to knock the gun out of Jesse's hand and then get his temper under control. "Jesse, getting us killed here on this road ain't going to help getting us the ranch back."

"But . . ."

"Just you simmer down, son. There is a time to fight and a time not to fight, and this is one of the times to shut up and not fight. Now let's cut the horse loose and do what they're tellin' us to do."

Jesse didn't like it, but his pa was making some sense. So he and Elias finally cut the harness free, and the skinny gelding climbed to its feet and wandered off into the sage-brush.

"Push it off the road!" a teamster yelled. "We ain't got all gawdamn day to wait on ya!"

Jesse was so hot and furious that he wanted to kill the man, but there were several others just as big and brutish, and they all had rifles at their sides. So he and Elias shoved their worthless old wagon off the road and watched it bounce down a dry ravine breaking all to pieces.

"I had that wagon nearly twenty years," Elias said as the dust at the bottom of the ravine settled. "It helped get us out here from Colorado."

"Well, good riddance to the damned thing! I was ashamed to be driving such a sad piece of shit and that old horse of yours wasn't making me feel any better."

"Someone will catch him up and fatten him," Elias argued. "I've been told many times that horses . . . even old ones . . . are worth real good money up here on the Comstock."

Jesse spat into the powdery dry dirt and then glared at the teamsters who had started moving again. "Let's go. Virginia City is just over the divide, and I need a drink and to find that son of a bitch Gardner."

"Now just you settle down a mite, Jesse. It's Dan that we ought to be lookin' for first."

"Dan can wait on a bottle of whiskey and our meeting with Gardner. When I see my kid brother, I want to be able to show him the deed to our ranch. I want to wave it in Dan's face and show him what his big brother has done for the family."

"I can almost see the light of pride showin' in Dan's eyes right now. And I'll sure as hell be glad to see him come out of those deep mines. Lot of men die down in the mines. I've heard that the cemetery hill has a new corpse added every day."

"Well, Dan isn't going to be one of them, by gawd!"

Jesse attacked the hill, leaving the old man to struggle along behind. When he topped the divide, he gazed at Virginia City with all its tall buildings and bustling activity as he waited for Elias, who finally joined him, looking pale and weak.

"Old age," Elias gasped, fighting hard for his breath, "is hell."

"Better'n dyin' young," Jesse told him as they started into Virginia City looking to find the rich man that had taken their ranch at a gawdamned auction sale.

# Chapter 24

Jesse and Elias spent the next few hours ordering drinks in the famous Bucket of Blood Saloon. The Bucket of Blood overlooked the Virginia & Truckee Railroad depot and then farther out on the barren, rocky hills, the Catholic, Protestant, and finally a shabby cemetery reserved for the whores, Chinese, Indians, and Mexicans, along with anyone else that was seen as being unworthy of being buried in the two "respectable" cemeteries.

As they sat by a big picture window looking out over the railroad, the huge mining operations, the lonely cemeteries, and a hundred miles of rolling sagebrush hills dotted with juniper and pinyon pines, Elias sighed and said, "The Comstock Lode would be a mighty, mighty hard place to live and die."

"That it is," Jesse agreed, watching a saloon girl as she poured a pitcher of beer into glasses at the next table. She had big breasts and they bulged out for everyone to see. "Hard. Hard."

Elias turned his eyes from the window and followed Jesse's eyes. "Forget it," he said. "She's probably got ten men waiting in line as soon as she leaves this job."

"Maybe she does, but if I wanted I could go to the head of her line."

Elias snorted. "You always did have a way with women. More often than not, they got you into trouble. Did you find any worthy of marrying like your mother?"

Jesse scowled and thought of Alice. "I found one that I actually did marry."

"You did!" The old man was all ears and suddenly excited. "What happened to her, Jesse? I'd have liked you to have brought her out here so's I could have met her. Dan would have liked to have met her, too. You goin' to bring her home to meet us?"

"Drink up and quit asking so many questions," Jesse snapped, reaching out and patting the barmaid on her plump butt.

"Hey! Watch your hands there, buster!"

"Sorry," he said, grinning.

She looked at him, and when she saw how good-looking Jesse was her frown disappeared. "Well, just watch yourself unless you're invited to handle the goods."

"I wouldn't mind handling them tonight," Jesse said, ignoring the looks of the beer drinkers. "What time are you off this saloon job?"

"Never mind that," one of the miners said. "Mabel has plenty to do after work. Ain't that right, Mabel, honey?"

The barmaid looked at the three rough miners and decided she had better nod her head. "Don't want any trouble here, boys."

Jesse chuckled. "Don't you worry about me getting hurt, Mabel. I could eat all three of those assholes for breakfast."

The three miners started to come to their feet and Jesse figured he would use his knife on them, but Mabel stepped in between and said, "Come on, boys. Let's keep things friendly, otherwise nobody gets to see Mabel after this shift. Understand?"

The miners understood and sat back down. Mabel turned to Jesse and said, "You sure know how to ignite a fuse of dynamite. Maybe you ought to find another place to drink with your old man."

"I like this one, but I am looking for someone. A fella named Thomas T. Gardner. You ever heard of him, Mabel?"

"Sure I have. He's an attorney with an office just down C Street. You'll see his sign hanging out there."

"Jesse," Elias pleaded, "let's go find Mr. Gardner before we get drunk and into trouble. Remember, we're here to get the ranch back, not get into a fight over a barroom floozy."

"Hey!" Mabel cried with mock exaggeration. "You ain't callin' me a 'floozy' now, are you?"

"No, ma'am," Elias Walker said. "And we were just leavin'."

As they got up to go and then passed the bar, Mabel hurried over and whispered to Jesse, "You could meet me after midnight when I'm not engaged. I'm staying at the . . ."

"Never mind," Jesse said coldly. "Why would I want to follow three dirty miners who had been humpin' you all evening?"

The insult was cruel and so unexpected that Mabel's eyes shot wide open and then she hissed, "You arrogant bastard!"

Jesse laughed, slapped Mabel's ass, and headed out of the Bucket of Blood. "Let's find Gardner and get the ranch bought back and then let's hook up with Dan and get him out of the mines. I can hardly wait to see the expression on his face when I tell him he's going to be a rancher again."

Five minutes later they were standing in the small but nicely furnished outer office of Thomas T. Gardner, Esq. "He must be doing pretty well," Jesse mused. "This is a real nice place."

"Sure is. I knew Mr. Gardner had loads of money," Elias said. "Wonder where he went?"

"I'll bet he's in his back office," Jesse said, walking over to the door and pushing it open without knocking.

"Hey!" a well-dressed man in his early fifties objected from behind a polished mahogany desk. "Don't you fellas know how to knock before entering?"

"I do for a fact," Jesse said, his eyes sweeping over the expensive furniture and oil paintings on the wall. "I guess you know my father, Elias Walker."

Elias had his hat off and pushed in behind Jesse. "Sorry for not knocking, Mr. Gardner."

The attorney waved his hand in dismissal. "Never mind, but I'm pretty busy today. I was just going over some documents for an upcoming court appearance. I'm representing the Ophir Mine in an accident case. One of its miners fell out of the cage halfway down the shaft. He fell almost eight hundred feet and there wasn't a lot left of him when they finally got to his body, which must have ricocheted off the shaft walls all the way down. The corpse was torn limb from limb. The thing of it was I have witnesses that will testify that the man was drunk when he climbed in the cage. That will absolve my client of all liability."

"Well good for you and bully for the Ophir Mine," Jesse said without even attempting to sound sincere. "But we're not here to listen to you brag about how you're going to help the rich stay rich . . . we're here to buy back our ranch."

Gardner blushed at the insult he'd just received, and he became all business. "Sorry, but I'm afraid that you are too late. I've just received an offer for the ranch and I'm working up a counteroffer that I think will result in a quick sale."

Jesse's jaw muscles corded in his cheeks and he closed the door behind them. "Forget about the counteroffer," he said bluntly.

"Beg your pardon?"

"I said that you have to sell it back to me and my family," Jesse told the attorney. "And you're gonna sell it for the same price you paid my father for it . . . three thousand dollars."

Thomas T. Gardner threw back his head and had a nice, brittle laugh. "How amusing! Do you really think I'd buy something that I couldn't make a nice profit on?"

"I don't care what kind of profit you expected," Jesse said, a hard edge coming into his voice. "We've come to buy it back. It's been ours for years. My father and late mother homesteaded that ranch and built it up from nothing with their sweat and blood. Now, it's coming back to us, and I've got the cash to get us back the deed."

Gardner steepled his soft white fingers and studied his manicure for a moment before he said, "You would be Jesse. Right?"

"That's right."

"I've heard a lot about you, Jesse. Now your younger brother Dan . . . well, no one says anything but good about the kid. But you. . . . well, let's just say that you're not a man I care to deal with."

Jesse took two steps forward and leaned hard on Gardner's desk, shoving his face forward, "You're gonna sell the ranch to me, Mr. Gardner, of that there is no doubt."

The attorney slid his chair back, and his eyes widened with the beginnings of fear. "Are you threatening me?"

Instead of answering, Jesse pulled out his wallet and counted three thousand dollars. "And there is an extra thousand for your profit."

"Not enough," Gardner told him. "Not nearly enough."

"Then what the hell is enough!"

The attorney forced a cold smile. "I can sell your former ranch at a profit of ten thousand dollars, minimum."

There was a long silence and then Elias blurted, "Mr. Gardner, are you telling us that the ranch is worth thirteen thousand dollars?"

"That's right. I'll have to put a little money into improvements, of course. Have some fencing redone and that well re-dug deeper. And the house is a pigsty, and it needs a thorough cleaning and some paint and fixing up, but yes, with a little investment on my part, I'll get at least thirteen thousand."

"Jesus," Jesse hissed. "You make that kind of a profit at the expense of my father, who spent most of his life struggling to make that ranch what it is today!"

"I'm a businessman, Mr. Walker. There is nothing personal to this . . . it's all about making money."

Jesse took a deep breath and then whispered, "But what good is money if you can't spend it, Mr. Gardner?"

The question rocked the attorney, and he jumped out of his chair and then reached into a drawer and dragged out a pistol. Pointing it at Jesse, he stammered, "Are you *threatening* my life?"

Jesse smiled and the wheels inside his head were spinning. "No, sir! I was just thinking that none of us know the exact hour of our departure from this world. But at the same time I was thinking something else that you might like to hear."

"I really doubt that you have anything that I'd like to hear," the attorney said, unable to hide a tremble in his voice.

Jesse began to count out the money, and when he got to fourteen thousand dollars he smiled broadly and said, "There it is. I've just beat the offer that you think you're gonna get by a thousand dollars, and you don't even have to invest a penny in the deal."

The attorney stared at the pile of cash. "You're willing to

pay me fourteen thousand dollars for a ranch I got for three thousand?"

"Like you said, you're in it for the money and it's not personal."

Gardner swallowed, and his hand moved involuntarily toward the stack of cash. His soft white fingers scooped it up, and he recounted the money and then he looked at Jesse and said, "A quick sale deed is what you want. I can write it up now, and we'll immediately have it notarized. There is an attorney that I work with right next door, and he'll do the notarization."

"Then let's get it done," Jesse said quietly. "My kid brother is probably killing himself down in some hot, stinking mineshaft, and I want to find him and get him back to where he belongs before he either gets hurt or killed."

"I understand!" Thomas T. Gardner was smiling again. He sat down and wrote out a quick sale deed for the property and gave it to Jesse saying, "I assume that you, Elias, and your brother Dan will all want to be listed on the deed as equal owners of the ranch."

Jesse could see no way to get around that fact even though he wanted it in his name only. But he could make that change later. "That's fine, Mr. Gardner."

"Good! If you have any questions or . . ."

"Quit your yappin' while I read this."

"Why, yes, Mr. Walker. Of course."

The deed was satisfactory. Short and simple with nothing in it that could be challenged in court or misinterpreted. "It's fine. Get your friend in here to notarize our signatures."

Moments later, the four of them were shaking hands and the deal was done. The other attorney, whose name Jesse didn't bother to recall, departed the office with a wink to his associate that left no doubt he was impressed with the sales price and the speed with which the ranch had been sold to its former owners.

Everyone seemed happy. Elias especially, but even Jesse. On their way out of the office and down the street to find Dan, Elias was fairly dancing and he looked ten years younger.

"I'm sorry you had to pay fourteen thousand dollars for the ranch. Yes, sir, I'm real sorry about that, but we'll build it up again and someday when I'm dead and gone it'll all belong to you and Dan and be worth a whole lot more than fourteen thousand."

"I'm sure you're right," Jesse said, eyes locked straight ahead as he carefully plotted how he was going to murder the attorney and get his money back before they left the Comstock Lode tomorrow morning.

# Chapter 25

Longarm and Alice had gotten a much needed rest on the train ride between Rock Springs and Reno. Arriving in Reno, they had spent the night at a beautiful hotel located beside the Truckee River, which flowed through the town. After an exciting night of frequent and energetic lovemaking, they had boarded a stagecoach for Carson City via Virginia City.

"I wish that we could go straight to Carson City without going through the Comstock Lode," Alice said as their stagecoach headed south. "Seems like an unnecessary detour."

"Carson City is Nevada's territorial capital," Longarm said, "but it's the Comstock that is the driver of all the wealth and industry in Western Nevada. And besides, Virginia City is pretty much in the same direction. It's just that it's quite a climb up onto the Comstock. Even so, we should be in Carson City early this evening."

"And then?"

"Then we find out exactly where the Walker Ranch is located, rent a buggy or a pair of horses tomorrow morning, and get Jesse."

She took Longarm's hand. "I'm scared to death. If we

find Jesse, I'm afraid that something will go wrong and he might kill you . . . or me. However, if we don't find him then . . . then what?"

"Sooner or later we'll find the man and bring him to justice," Longarm promised. "So just relax. I have been thinking that you probably ought to remain in Carson City while I go out to the ranch and . . ."

"Oh, no! I'm not letting you go out there alone to face Jesse and his family. Uh-uh! We're in this together all the way."

Longarm knew better than to argue. Besides, he'd given her his gun while they were in Elko, waiting for their train to take on fuel and water as they'd walked out past the stock pens. Longarm had needed to see if Alice really could shoot straight, and she'd proven that she was an excellent shot. That had reassured him that she could hold her own if the bullets started flying because he already knew that Alice was brave.

There were three other passengers on the stagecoach when it departed Reno, but no one seemed inclined toward conversation. The road up onto Sun Mountain was steep and heavily trafficked mostly by ore and supply wagons, and there was a steady stream of miners walking up the mountain as well as others on horseback.

When they finally did roll down Virginia City's main street Alice was amazed at how big the place was and how massive were the mine works. "I never dreamed I'd see so much up here!"

"I've heard that there are so many miles of mine tunnels under Virginia City that, if they stretched them all out, you could walk underground from here to Sacramento," Longarm told her. "Some of these mines have shafts that go straight down well over a thousand feet. At those depths the air gets so hot that the miners are issued one hundred pounds of ice per shift, and they say that it feels like working in the depths of hell."

"Why do they do it?"

"The miner's union wages are very high, and some of the big mines give bonuses that can amount to a lot of money. A lot of these workers already were hard-rock miners from places like Wales."

"Virginia City is not as big as Denver," Alice said, "but it's still like a whole 'nother world."

"It's a boomtown, and it's wild and dangerous," Longarm told her. "It's not a place for a lady."

"I'm glad that we're just passing through," Alice admitted. "But now that I've seen it I'm also glad that we did come this way."

"I thought you'd be impressed."

As their stagecoach navigated C Street congested with people, wagons, horses, and mules Longarm and Alice were gawking at everything I sight. But it was Alice who cried out in shock. "That's him! That's *Jesse!*"

"Where!"

"He and two men went up that side street," Alice shouted, pointing frantically up the congested mountainside with its narrow dirt roads and closely packed buildings.

Longarm hadn't seen Jesse, but he was sure that Alice hadn't made a mistake. If it were true, they had gotten very lucky and this manhunt was about to end one way or the other.

"Driver!" Longarm shouted, sticking his head out of the coach. "Stop! Driver!"

But there was so much clamor and noise not only from barking dogs, baying mules, and loud piano music pouring out of every saloon that the driver simply couldn't hear him.

Longarm threw open the stagecoach's door. "Up that side street? Is that where you saw them disappear?"

"Yes, but . . ."

Longarm jumped out of the moving stagecoach. The street was muddy from a recent rain and he slipped and fell headfirst into a big puddle. The pale brown mud had a lot of adobe in it and it stuck to him like paste.

"Wait!" Alice cried, jumping after him and landing face-first in the mud and water. "Oh my gawd! Look at us!"

Longarm helped her up. "Maybe it's better that we look this way," he grunted. "With our faces covered with this damned, clinging mud, Jesse will be slow to recognize either of us. Come on, let's catch up to them!"

They ran up the side street, but there was no sign of Jesse or his two companions. Longarm grabbed Alice's hand, and they charged up to a higher intersection, and when he turned toward the Piper's Opera House, there was Jesse and his two companions moving along at a leisurely pace. Jesse was in the middle of the trio, his big arms draped over the shoulders of his companions.

Longarm wiped the mud off his hands and dragged out his gun. Alice did the same. They raced after the three men, who were laughing together, and when Longarm got to within fifteen feet he shouted, "That's far enough, Walker!"

Jesse spun around and when he saw Longarm and Alice his hand streaked for his gun. Longarm didn't hesitate an instant as he shot the man four times in the chest, watching as Jesse backpedaled with his arms windmilling wildly. Alice stood frozen until the old man started to pull out his gun, and when he did she cried, "No!"

But Elias Walker was either hard of hearing or he was prepared to die because he fired off one wild round as both Longarm and Alice shot him dead.

The last of the three men screamed in rage and not being armed, he charged Longarm and Alice. He was big, young, and crazy with grief. Longarm planted his feet and when the kid was almost on top of him he laid the barrel of his pistol across the kid's head and dropped him as if he'd been axed.

"Oh my gawd!" Alice cried. "Oh my gawd, we killed Jesse and his father!"

Longarm nodded. "We think that's exactly what we did."

"It happened so fast that . . ."

"I know," Longarm said quietly. "Sometimes it ends that way. Just so fast that you don't even have time to think . . . only to act. But it's done."

She went to Jesse's side and tears dripped from her eyes to fall on his dirty, whisker-stubbled face. "You had it all, Jesse. You had me and money and . . . we could have made a good life together, damn you!"

Longarm could think of nothing that he could do or say that would ease her grief. Jesse Walker had been evil . . . a cold-blooded killer and a thief. He had deserved to die hard and slow instead of fast and easy as had been his fate. As for the old man, it didn't matter. In Longarm's experience the father was often the cause of evil in a son and that meant that the youngest one lying unconscious with a gash in his scalp and blood running down his face probably should have also died.

"Alice," he said, "I saw a doctor's office down on C Street. I'm going to carry the kid down there and see if I killed him or not. You can come along . . . or stay."

Instead of answering, she searched Jesse's pockets and found a whole lot of cash . . . not nearly as much as he'd stolen from her grandfather, but a lot. And she also discovered a deed to the Walker Ranch dated and notarized that very day. And last, she found her grandfather's beloved gold nugget.

"Look," she said, crying softly.

"Jesse was no good, Alice. No good at all."

"I know," she whispered. "Maybe all three of these men were evil."

"Maybe."

Longarm searched the old man's pockets but found nothing of worth. He picked up the unconscious young man he had just pistol-whipped and started for the doctor's office, knowing he'd really hit the kid hard. Hard enough to kill him or damage his brain beyond repair. Maybe he'd taken it out on the kid because he was related to Jesse Walker . . . as if they were a pair of poisonous snakes. But the kid hadn't even been armed, and he was dressed in miner's clothing. His hands were heavily calloused, and it was obvious that he was a hardworking man.

Maybe he was even a good and honest man.

# Chapter 26

Jesse's kid brother, Dan, had survived the vicious pistol-whipping up in Virginia City. After a few days when he'd regained consciousness and the doctor thought he'd be able to travel in a carriage, they'd taken him down to his ranch along with Jesse and Elias to be buried. In the days that followed, Longarm watched Alice care for Dan, and he saw something that he had not expected. The kid was not a bad kid . . . instead he was a good, honest, and forgiving man. They'd told him about Jesse and the murders and robberies. They'd shown him the big gold nugget and he'd explained everything about the new deed that Jesse had purchased from Thomas T. Gardner for their family cattle ranch.

"I guess it belongs to me now," Dan said one morning as he gazed out at the land. "It's where my family is buried . . . and where they belong, but I'll sell it back to Mr. Gardner and give you the money that was stolen from your grandfather, Alice."

"You said your father only got three thousand dollars for this ranch at auction. That's almost like stealing a place this nice."

Dan nodded. "I know."

"What is it really worth?" Alice asked.

"Jesse told me that the lawyer said he was going to be offered thirteen thousand, so that's why Jesse offered fourteen."

"Then that's probably what it is worth."

"I guess," Dan said, eyes fixed on the family burial plots. "This land has water and good grass. I got a feeling that the drought is over and things are going to turn around."

"And you think this place will make a good living off cattle and horses?"

"Yeah, it would if it is restocked. Our fencing needs work and the well has to be deepened. But I could have done those things myself. I was trying to earn enough money up at the mine to save to buy materials. Pa and I talked all the time about what it would take to fix this ranch up nice even when it didn't belong to us anymore."

"It does now," Alice said. "You are the only living person on the deed."

"Yeah, sure, but I . . ."

Alice sighed. "I don't have anything left in Denver but bad memories. And I always loved animals and dreamed of ranching."

Both Longarm and Dan were sitting on the front porch of the ranch house staring at Alice, wondering where she was going with this. "Dan," she said, "I can get Gardner or another attorney to represent me, and because this place was bought by your brother with stolen money I'm sure the courts would take it away from you again."

"I know."

"Or," Alice said, "we can keep the ranch and be partners. All three of us as equal partners."

"Whoa!" Longarm exclaimed. "I don't want to be a rancher."

"I do," Alice said, slapping her hands together. "What about it, Dan? Do you still want to be a rancher or would you rather go back to the mines up on the Comstock Lode?"

"I love ranching," he said simply. "It's all that I've ever wanted to do."

"Then that's it," Alice said with a firm nod of her chin. "I'll let my grandmother know that we'll work out something with her, and we'll stay and make a go of things right here on this beautiful ranch."

"You and me?" Dan asked, looking nearly dumbfounded.

"You're a good man, aren't you, Dan Walker?"

He blushed. "Some would tell you so."

"Well, I'm a betrayed bride but I'm still a good woman," Alice said quietly. "And this is where I'm going to make my stand."

And then, as a slow grin began to spread across Longarm's handsome face, he watched as Alice Walker and Dan Walker shook hands on what he bet would be a loving and lifetime partnership.